PUSH

MOON

'A novel so close to perfection that, as a
writer, I was immediately engulfed by
conflicting feelings of both jealousy and
awe over its achievements… Exemplary…
As historically valuable as it is powerful,
as poetic as it is horrific. It is a treasure'

BENJAMIN MYERS

'Llamazares has written a great lyrical
story… This tale is one that should
be read aloud around the campfire'

LA VOZ DE GALICIA

JULIO LLAMAZARES (b. 1955) is a poet, novelist, essayist, journalist and screenwriter, whose work has been translated into over twenty languages. He has twice been a finalist for Spain's National Literature Prize, for *Wolf Moon* (1985) and *The Yellow Rain* (1988).

SIMON DEEFHOLTS and KATHRYN PHILLIPS-MILES both studied Romance Languages and Literature at University College of Wales, Aberystwyth, and later at Birkbeck College, University of London. They have jointly translated several novels and plays, and they live and work in Spain.

BENJAMIN MYERS is the author of eleven novels. These include *Cuddy*, winner of the 2023 Goldsmiths Prize, *The Gallows Pole*, adapted for the screen, and the international best-seller *The Offing*. His latest novel is *Jesus Christ Kinski*.

WOLF MOON

JULIO LLAMAZARES

TRANSLATED FROM THE SPANISH
BY SIMON DEEFHOLTS AND
KATHRYN PHILLIPS-MILES

FOREWORD BY BENJAMIN MYERS

PUSHKIN PRESS CLASSICS

Pushkin Press
Somerset House, Strand
London WC2R 1LA

Wolf Moon was first published as *Luna de lobos* by Seix Barral in Barcelona, 1985

The afterword, 'Muere el héroe de mi infancia' ('My Childhood Hero
Has Died'), was first published in *La Crónica de León* (6 June 2004)
and a revised version reprinted in *Entre perro y lobo* in 2008.

First published in Great Britain by Peter Owen Publishers in 2017
First published by Pushkin Press in 2024
This edition published in 2025

ISBN 13: 978-1-80533-321-0

Cover image © Superstock/Iberfoto Archivo.
Excursionistes: Sigueu prudents amb el foc!
by Evarist Móra i Rosselló for the Forest Service of Generalitat de Catalunya

The authorised representative in the EEA is
eucomply OÜ, Pärnu mnt. 139b-14, 11317, Tallinn, Estonia,
hello@eucompliancepartner.com, +33757690241

Offset by Tetragon, London
Printed and bound in the United Kingdom by Clays Ltd, Elcograf S.p.A.

Pushkin Press is committed to a sustainable future for our
business, our readers and our planet. This book is made from
paper from forests that support responsible forestry.

MIX
Paper | Supporting
responsible forestry
FSC® C018072

www.pushkinpress.com

1 3 5 7 9 8 6 4 2

CONTENTS

FOREWORD

I find that in these situations it is always best to be honest: I wandered into *Wolf Moon* blindly. With no prior of knowledge of either the novel or its creator Julio Llamazares, I resisted that ever-present modern urge to turn to the internet for the merest snippet of information or a signpost that might at least give me a hint as to the kind of literary territory I was about to enter.

But I stood firm with only the phrase "We think you'll like this…" echoing through my mind as I cracked the spine for the first time. What lay within was one of those rare discoveries – a novel so close to perfection that, as a writer, I was immediately engulfed by conflicting feelings of both jealousy and awe over its achievements.

Wolf Moon could – let us say *should* – be considered a pursuit novel that has earned its place alongside some of the best in a genre that seemed to increase after the publication in 1915 of John Buchan's genre defining *The Thirty-Nine Steps*. A pursuit novel is exactly as it suggests: a high stakes game of cat and mouse, where nothing less than life, death and liberty are the prevailing themes. It can take place in any country in any era, and against any political backdrop, though two world wars certainly broadened its potential for possible new plot lines. And while, superficially at least, the pursuit novel appears to belong to the thriller section of the bookshop, the best examples are simply stand-alone works of classic literature which once read are rarely forgotten. These are the archetypal page-turners – a description that, to my mind at least, is the highest praise that can be bestowed upon a writer's work.

Published in 1939, *Rogue Male* by Geoffrey Household and a comparable but lesser-known novel that preceded it in 1936, *Wild Harbour* by the Scottish author Ian McPherson, both seemed to prophesise the experience of many who would find themselves having to flee Nazi persecution via gripping heart-in-mouth accounts. Tellingly, though neither name the threat, all readers coming to such works implicitly understand the historical context. No one needs the dire and depraved deeds of Hitler and his cohorts explaining to them to appreciate why capture by them must be evaded.

And so too *Wolf Moon* belongs to a world where the emphasis is placed upon the pursued rather than the regime itself from which they are fleeing. A reader need not know the intricacies of the Spanish Civil War in order to immerse themselves in the experience that Llamazares relates. And it *is* an experience, with each dank cave, miserable downpour or starvation pang keenly felt. This is not the Spain of sun, sea and sangria that we know in Britain, but rather a place of fear, fascism and permanent flight. (Reading it now, I am also reminded of other tonally similar works, such as the Booker nominated *Figures In A Landscape* by Barry England or, more recently, *A Meal In Winter* and *Four Soldiers* by Hubert Mingarelli.)

In it we join four beleaguered and fearful fugitives retreating to the Cantabrian Mountains, which run from east to west across the northern region of Spain. Today the mountains are a popular spot for hiking, skiing and the undertaking of particularly challenging climbing routes, but following the Republican defeat at the hands of fascistic Francisco Franco's Guardia Civil during the Spanish Civil War of 1936 to 1939, they also provided a topographical sanctuary in which the anarchist survivors could hole up, regroup or just simply stay alive. 420,000 Spaniards were killed during this period and as the narrative careers onwards we can't help but wonder what ultimate fates await Gildo, Ramiro, Juan and narrator Ángel, each young man already tainted by the trauma of violence while bringing risk to those friends and family left tantalising close by in their home villages, and who they attempt to make contact with in scenes that are nothing less than heartbreaking. No reader with a heart could scour such sections and not put themselves in their positions. There but for the grace of God go I…

The writing is exemplary as Llamazares lures us in with pure poetry. In *Wolf Moon* a bell does not simply ring, it instead grinds out "four peals of wounded iron that explode into the night, showering my heart with something bitter, cold and mineral". Elsewhere, "light lashes the immense darkness of the earth's entrails like a bloody knife". Or how about this for a sentence: "the water suppurating from the depths of the mine spirals into a puddle of its own neglect, forming a dirty spring, a foul-smelling stream trickle through the heaps of rubble."

This is writing of the highest order, and made all the more effective by the knowledge that this is human history. It may be a fictional rendering, but never once do we doubt the veracity of the world that Llamazares relates. This actually happened, we tell ourselves. This actually happened within living memory, and we allowed it.

As the story progresses we also find ourselves increasingly trapped in the sodden and sometimes snow-bound hostile mountain range, where morsels of food rot in the damp, the only inhabitants of abandoned buildings are "solitude and neglect" (neglect of space, of purpose, or people) and the landscape itself becomes the unforgiving and indifferent central character, unable to do anything but passively observe the human cruelty that plays across it.

If you hold this book in your hands then you don't need persuading to read it. Nor do you need the plot giving away – a fatal error of any novel's foreword. But before you do, let us remember that following his victory over the Republican proletariat, Franco ruled as dictatorial leader of Spain for another 35 years, his torrid reign only coming to an end shortly before his death in 1975. To understand the true impact of his decades-long campaigns of terror, we turn to poetry and fiction. We turn to a novel such as *Wolf Moon* to free ourselves from cold historic fact and instead allow ourselves to experience those raw emotions of its characters. We know we can never truly understand the plight of these resistance heroes, but we can at least sympathise and pray such regimes do not rise again, even if we must begrudgingly concede the grim reality that comparable situations are happening in the world right now. Like the best book about politics, *Wolf Moon* draws the Spanish Civil War away from dictatorial dogma and party factions and instead brings it down to something far more important and enduring: humanity.

Across the terse, pared-down narrative Llamazares takes us through four time periods running from 1937 to 1946, each section becoming a little more exhausting, desperate and lonely than that which has gone before. But he also delivers an afterword that allows some light to shine through one of the worst periods of European history; hope is here, finally, late in the day. Meanwhile, no word is wasted throughout, leaving this reader reeling at the revelations within.

Literature's purpose is to tell these stories and in *Wolf Moon* we have a novel that is as historically valuable as it is powerful, as poetic as it is horrific. It is a treasure.

Benjamin Myers

WOLF
MOON

Part One
1937

Part One

1937

1

As evening falls, the wood grouse is singing in the nearby beech groves. The cold *cierzo* wind suddenly stops, wraps itself around the trees' sore branches and tears off the last few autumn leaves. Then the black rain, which has been lashing the mountains violently for several days, finally stops.

*

Ramiro is sitting by the door of the shepherd's hut where we took refuge the night before last, fleeing from the rain and from death. As he squeezes the cigarette I have just rolled for him between his fingers, morosely and ritualistically, he stares intently at the trail of rocks and mud that the downpour has washed down the side of the mountain. His silhouette is outlined in the doorway against the milky-grey half-light of the evening sky, like the profile of an animal that is motionless, perhaps dead.

'Well,' he says. 'It looks like it's over.' He glances towards the corner where his brother Juan, Gildo and I are huddled up next to the fire, burning bitter green wood, trying unsuccessfully to avoid the rain leaking in through the roof. 'As soon as night falls we'll cross the mountain pass,' says Ramiro, lighting his cigarette. 'We'll be on the other side by dawn.'

Gildo smiles behind his balaclava, his grey eyes shining. He throws a bundle of branches on to the fire. The flames spring up, warm and cheerful, in the spiral of smoke that rises to meet the rain soaking through the thatched roof.

*

The moon has not come out tonight either. The night is like a cold black stain on the outline of the beech groves, which climb up the mountain and into the fog like ghostly armies of ice. It smells of rosemary and shredded ferns.

Our boots slosh through the mud searching for the elusive surface of the ground with each step. Our submachine-guns shine in the darkness like iron moons.

We carry on climbing towards the Amarza Pass, towards the roof of the world and solitude.

*

Suddenly, Ramiro stops in the middle of the heather. He sniffs the night like an injured wolf. With his one and only hand, he points into the distance.

'What's up?' asks Gildo, his voice barely a murmur in the fog's frozen lament.

'Up there. Can't you hear it?'

The northerly *cierzo* wind blows down the mountain, whipping through the heather and the silence. It fills the night with its howl.

'It's the *cierzo*,' I tell him.

'No, it's not the *cierzo*, it's a dog. Can you hear it now?'

I can now. I can hear it clearly, a sad distant barking, like a groan. A barking that the fog stretches and drags down the hill.

Gildo takes his submachine-gun off his shoulder without

making a sound. 'At this time of year there are no shepherds still up in the passes,' he says.

The four of us now have our weapons in our hands, and, motionless, we listen out for the sudden crack of a branch or an isolated word in the *cierzo*, scanning the mountain for a still shadow waiting in ambush in the fog.

We hear the barking again, more clearly now, in front of us. There is no doubt about it. A dog is chewing the frozen entrails of the night up in the pass.

*

The barking has guided us through the darkness, along the path that crosses through fields of heather and broom, towards the grey line of the horizon.

We are close now. Ramiro signals. Juan, Gildo and I deploy quickly to either side. The climb is now much slower and more difficult, without the dark outline of the path to guide us and with thick undergrowth gripping our feet like animals' claws buried in the mud.

Ramiro's shadow on the path has stopped again. Now the dog is barking just a few metres away from us.

On the grey line of the horizon, behind a line of oak trees, we can make out the shadow of a rooftop, imprecise and frozen, floating in the fog.

The shelter and sheepfold at the top of the pass are a mass of crumbling dry-stone walls. A strong smell of excrement and neglect assaults our noses. A smell of solitude.

The barking threatens to blow apart the night's swollen belly.

'Is anyone there?' Gildo's voice rumbles in the silence like damp gunpowder. It forces both the dog and the wind to be quiet, at the same time. 'Hey, is anyone there?'

Again, silence. Dense and profound. Indestructible.

The door creaks bitterly as it turns on its hinges. Like it's half-asleep. The beam of Gildo's torch slowly ruptures the heavy darkness inside the shelter. Nothing. There is no one there. Only the terrified eyes of the dog in the corner.

Ramiro and Juan come out from behind the oak trees and approach the shelter.

'There's no one here,' says Gildo.

'What about the dog?'

'I don't know. It's in here. On its own. Scared to death.'

A barely perceptible moan comes from the corner, which is lit up again in the torchlight.

Juan goes up to the dog cautiously. 'OK, OK. Don't be afraid. Where's your owner?'

The animal cowers in the straw, its eyes full of panic.

'He's got a broken leg,' says Juan. 'They must have abandoned him.'

Ramiro puts his pistol back in its holster. 'Kill it. Don't leave it to suffer any longer.' Juan looks at his brother incredulously. 'It's what the owner should have done before he left,' says Ramiro, collapsing heavily on to a pile of straw.

*

The straw is soaking wet, compacted by the damp. It compresses under my body like soft bread. Outside, the *cierzo* still beats violently against the heather and the oak trees. It howls over the roof of the shelter and goes off down the mountain in search of the night's memory.

Opposite the open door, hanging from a branch, the swollen black body of the dog swings gently back and forth.

*

Someone has lit a lamp in the farmhouse at the bottom of the valley, which nestles peacefully in the foothills of the southern slope of the pass. The babbling of the newborn river greets us, together with the gentle sound of the breeze in the willow groves.

It will soon be dawn. It will soon be dawn and, by then, we will have to be hidden away. Daylight is not good for dead men.

'I'll go down first,' says Ramiro, getting up from the stone wall he has been sitting on. 'You three stay next to the river and cover the retreat. OK?'

Gildo and Juan stamp their thick boots on the wet grass, trying to shake off the cold.

Slowly, we begin to descend towards the valley, its higher fields climbing uphill to meet us.

The river is swollen by the rains of the past few days. It roars lugubriously under the wooden bridge that Ramiro has just crossed in a low crouch, slowly, not making a sound. Like a hunter who, over time, has come to imitate the animal movements of his quarry.

But the dogs have already caught his scent, and it is not long before the outline of a man, alerted by their barking, appears in the window, which pours a torrent of crimson light on to the water.

Ramiro flattens himself against the wall of the farmhouse. 'Who's there?'

The man's voice reaches us, muffled by the frost on the windows and the river's roar.

Ramiro does not reply.

Now, a second figure, a woman, appears at the window. They seem to be arguing while, fearfully, they scan the shadows of the night in front of the house. Then they both disappear, and a moment later the light goes out. Beside me, in the willow groves, Gildo and Juan are watching, restless and impatient.

A door. The creak of a door. And a voice shouting across the river, 'Don't move or I'll shoot.'

The three of us charge across the bridge towards the house. The barking in the yard gets louder.

When we get there Ramiro's pistol is pointing at the face of a man gripped by terror and the cold.

*

Some milk is bubbling on the stove in an old blackened saucepan, filling the kitchen with steam. The stove is still just about warm, and the crackling of the burning logs and the spirals of pungent red smoke drive out the cold of the night and the memory of the rain. The four of us are eating now. Our weapons are propped, forgotten, against the back of the bench, and our memories are pervaded by the familiar flavours of earlier times. We've had nothing to eat for five days.

The woman, wrapped up in a black shawl and her hair tied back carelessly, places the saucepan of milk in the middle of the table and goes back to stand by the hearth next to her husband. She is slim, with fair hair and light-brown eyes, still pretty despite the sadness that lies deep behind her smudged lips and hugely swollen belly. She has not said a single word since she came into the kitchen. She has not even looked at us.

Ramiro finishes his food and leans back against the bench.

'Does anyone else live here?' he asks the couple.

'Not any more,' the man replies. 'The children are in La Moraña with their grandparents. It's safer there. And the lad is up in the hills with the cows.'

'When is he back?'

'Tomorrow.'

Gildo pours the milk on to his plate and watches as a red border forms around the edges. 'I used to like doing that when I was a kid,' he says, smiling.

The milk is hot and thick. It burns like fire as it goes down my throat.

The first light of dawn is now curling through the window shutter. It is white and bittersweet, like the steam from the milk which fills the kitchen.

'OK,' says Ramiro, getting up and going to the window. 'We'll sleep here today, and we'll be on our way again once it gets dark. You carry on with your chores as if nothing out of the ordinary has happened,' he adds, speaking to the owners of the farmhouse. 'And be careful. One of us will be watching you all the time.'

The man nods silently without even daring to look up from the floor.

But finally the woman bursts into tears. I can barely understand what she is saying as she fights back her sobs. 'But what have we done, for God's sake? What have we done? We've given you food. You've had food to eat and you've warmed up by the fire. Now go and leave us in peace. It's not our fault what's happening to you.'

The woman has collapsed on the bench, crying, burying her face in her hands. I can hear the bitter murmur of her weeping and see her enormous belly trembling beside me.

Her husband watches her from the hearth, scared and disconcerted, waiting for us to react.

It is Ramiro who reacts. He has taken out his pistol and orders the man to go to the door. We pick up our capes and our weapons and follow him in silence.

Before leaving, I turn around again to look at the woman, who is still crying on the bench, more softly now. I'd like to tell her that nothing is going to happen to them. I'd like to tell her that what's happening to us is not our fault either. But I know that it would be pointless.

2

We walk across the mountains for two long nights without stopping to rest, in search of the home we left a year ago.

We sleep by day, hidden in the undergrowth, and when night falls, when the shadows begin to stretch out across the sky, we start off again, hungry and tired.

Behind us, asleep in the depths of the moonlit valleys, we leave behind villages and hamlets, sheepfolds and farmhouses, barely discernible lights, fainting away in the night, on old river courses or under the desolate, vertical shelter of the mountains.

Until, little by little, the sky and the paths and the forests become familiar. Until, at last, having finally crossed the black peaks of Mount Morana, the distant rooftops of La Llánava appear before us, beneath the October night studded with stars and blueberry bushes, at the start of the wide valley streaked with poplar groves, carved out by the River Susarón at the foot of Mount Illarga.

*

'Look over there, Ángel. Beside the mill.' Ramiro crawls through the heather to hand me the binoculars. My eyes are instantly flecked with greens and yellows: water meadows next to the river, rows of elms, smoke rising lazily from the chimneys on the old rooftops of La Llánava. In a flood of bundled images – cows and winding paths, bridges, towers, backyards and alleyways, figures already stooping over in their vegetable plots – the familiar sights that I have never forgotten come flooding back to me from afar through the binoculars.

'On the path,' says Ramiro, pointing impatiently. 'By the dam. Can't you see her?'

Between the hedgerows that border the road to the mill, against the languid early morning mist, I finally spot a patch of yellow. A scarf.

'It's my sister!'

'Yes, it's Juana. She must be taking the cows out to the pasture at Las Llamas.'

Now I can see her, clear as crystal. She is walking slowly alongside the mill race carrying a cattle-goad, with her yellow scarf snatching at the morning light. I remember that scarf. I bought it for her myself, out of my first pay packet, so she could wear it when she came back from the threshing floor on the cart loaded with straw and lazy sunshine.

'I'm going down,' I say, my mind made up.

'Now?'

'Right now.'

Ramiro scans the whole valley again through the binoculars. 'It's too risky,' he says. 'Someone might see you from down below.'

'Not if I'm careful and stay in the undergrowth. I'll speak to Juana so they can get ready, and tonight all four of us will go down.'

I take off my cape, and Gildo hides it in the heather.

'Leave the submachine-gun here,' says Ramiro, passing me his handgun. 'It'll be easier with this.'

The three of them watch me leave in silence, anxious that someone might spot me. The area is occupied, full of soldiers, and our lives are now totally dependent upon how successful we are at not being seen.

*

Juana has turned around, startled, on the other side of the hedgerow where she had been sitting.

She jumps up and, without turning around again, begins to retrace her steps very slowly towards the middle of the field where the cows are grazing, bored and indifferent.

'Juana, Juana! Don't be scared, Juana. It's me, Ángel.' My voice is nothing more than a whisper among the brambles, but Juana hears me and stops suddenly, as if struck by a bullet.

Her blue eyes are wide open like two round coins, startled, incredulous, staring into mine.

'Sit down. Sit down where you were. With your back to me, like you were before. And look over at the cows.'

She does as I say and sits down again on the other side of the hedgerow, barely half a metre from where I'm lying flat on the ground, waiting for her. If I wanted to, I could almost reach out and touch her.

'What are you doing here?' she asks with a mixture of terror and tenderness in her voice. 'They'll kill you, Ángel. They'll kill you.'

'How is everyone?'

'We're fine,' she replies in a low voice. 'We thought we'd never see you again.'

'Well, here I am. Tell Father.'

'Did you come on your own?'

'No. I'm with Ramiro and his brother and Gildo from Candamo. You know who I mean; he got married to Lina. They are waiting up on the hillside.' My sister listens without turning her head, anxiously scratching at the ground with her goad. 'Listen, Juana. Tell Father that we'll come down into La Llánava tonight. Tell him to meet us in the hayloft. Make us something to eat. And if you can, go and see Ramiro's mother. We need to find somewhere to hide for a few days.'

In the distance, along the path by the river, some cows begin to low.

'Please go, Ángel, go. They'll kill you.' Juana has turned to face me, her eyes burning with fear. Her yellow scarf is like a sudden blaze of flames. 'They'll kill you,' she says again. 'They'll kill you.'

As I leave her, crawling through the heather like a mangy dog, her words still echo in my ears.

*

The moon has appeared from between the clouds, and it bathes the branches of the oak trees with frozen silver. Today a thick silence holds up the sky's dome, like an arch of black water curving gently over the valley.

Just beyond the oak groves, near the hill, is the start of a path. It is a drovers' path, which wends its way downhill between stone walls and fields of thyme. It is seeking out the roar of the river that runs down the mountain on the left, with bulrushes swaying in the distance. Further on, across the bridge, the roofs of La Llánava hack enormous chunks of black pulp out of the skyline.

*

The streets are empty. Not even the dogs, penned in by the *cierzo* wind against the warm languidness of the stables, seem to notice our arrival.

14

'Let's cross by the weir,' says Ramiro, at the head of the group, holding his handgun. 'It might be risky on the bridge.'

Down below, in among the willows and the reeds along the bank, the river's roar grows until it smashes against the arches of the bridge, against the old stones eaten away by water and time.

'You cross first, Ángel,' says Ramiro, keeping watch from the other riverbank.

The stones of the weir, which channels the water off towards the mill, are as slippery as sleeping fish beneath my boots. Like the skin of those trout we used to catch when we were boys, in the sleepy summer afternoons, while the villagers watched us from the bridge.

I make it across to the other bank. The grass here, next to the allotments, is overgrown, bursting with black nettles that bleed under my feet.

Motionless, holding my breath, I spend a few moments scanning the shadows of the closest allotments, the *cierzo* whistling between the hazels and the fruit trees. I make a signal, and immediately Gildo appears on the other side of the weir. He moves slowly, very slowly, testing the slippery surface of the stones with each step. His shadow shines on the surface of the water like the reflection of a tree rooted in the middle of the river.

Suddenly, I hear footsteps approaching the bridge. I'm showered with grass, and my mouth fills with lumps of bitter soil. I look out from under the pile of vegetation, which is almost pinning me to the ground. I reach for the submachine-gun. I look for Gildo's dark silhouette, now motionless, like a shadow on the weir. Up ahead the river is suddenly silent, as if it has died.

The approaching footsteps are now clearly audible. Backlit by the sky, two shadows pass along the parapet of the bridge, a man and a horse. They cross the bridge and continue on their way. They are lost in the night with a dull clattering of hooves.

On the weir, the river and Gildo start moving again.

*

It is pitch black in the hayloft. It almost hurts your eyes. The only sound is the fragrant dry crunch of the straw and the cows' heavy breathing as they sleep, beneath us, in the stable.

The silvery-black backdrop of the night disappears behind the door.

'Father?'

'Over here, Ángel, by the hatch.'

It's not my father's voice; it's my sister's, from the other end of the hayloft.

The grass is matted as it grows up towards the roof-beams. I feel her cold hand reaching for me in the darkness.

'Don't be afraid, Juana, don't be afraid.'

'Who's that with you?'

'Relax, Juana. It's Ramiro. Where's Father? Why hasn't he come?'

'He's not here. They took him off this afternoon.'

My sister collapses into my arms, barely able to stand, and bursts into tears. I can feel the burning tremor of her breast against mine and the salty and bitter caress of her tears.

'Who did? The Guardia Civil?'

'Yes. They took him to the barracks. Please, Ángel, leave. Leave now or they'll kill you.'

I hear a crunch of straw beside me and some footsteps. It's Ramiro.

'Hello, Juana.'

But she can't reply. Her tears and her mouth are drowning in my cape.

'They've taken away my father,' I tell Ramiro.

'Your father? Do they know you're here?'

My sister looks up from my shoulder. 'No, they don't know,' she says, fighting back the tears. 'They come by every so often. They search the houses and take a few of us away. The ones who've got family at the front.'

'Did you tell my mother?' Ramiro asks.

'I didn't have time. The *guardias* came. They searched the whole village, house by house.'

'Don't worry, Juana. Don't worry,' I say, trying to calm her down. 'Nothing's going to happen to Father, you'll see. He'll be back before you know it. And you can let Ramiro's mother know tomorrow. What you should do now is go back to bed. The *guardias* might come back with Father at any time.'

'What about you?'

'Don't worry about us, Juana. They'll never find us on the mountain.'

My sister has stopped crying. Only her intermittent breathing betrays her presence in the darkness. Before she goes she tells us more. 'Last night they killed Benito, the cartwright. Be careful, Ángel, be very careful.'

Once my sister has disappeared through the hatch between the hayloft and the stable, I search for Ramiro in the darkness. He calls out to me from the door.

'Come on, Ángel. What are you doing?'

'I'm going to wait here.'

'What? Are you crazy?'

'They've arrested my father. Don't you understand?'

'Of course I understand, Ángel, of course I do.' Although he tries to disguise it, Ramiro cannot hide the anxiety in his voice. 'They've taken your father to the barracks. So what? They'll ask him a few questions and let him go again.'

'I don't care,' I say, resolutely. 'I want to know what happens, and I'm going to wait for him.'

Ramiro hesitates for a moment then says, 'Fine, Ángel, you know what you're doing. I'm not going to force you. But remember that if they catch you they won't give you a second chance. Your sister's just told you what they did to Benito, and he was a lot less involved than we are.' Then, as he walks towards the door, he adds, 'Stay in the hayloft until your father gets back. If they searched the whole village this afternoon, they're not going to search it again now.' Ramiro gently opens the old wooden door and peers through the crack for a few seconds. 'We'll wait for you on the hillside,' he says.

Then he disappears into the vegetable garden where his brother and Gildo are waiting, keeping watch.

When Ramiro has gone I pull the door to and put the bar across it. Then I find a pitchfork and make a deep hole in the middle of the pile of hay. I jump in, cover myself with my cape and use the pitchfork to pull down an avalanche of hay on top of myself.

It is now completely impossible to breathe here in the darkness. But even if they prod the hay from one end to another with sticks and scythes they won't be able to find me.

*

Around two in the morning I wake with a start to the creaking of a heavy door on its hinges. It's a hoarse sound, muffled by the hay, out in the yard.

I listen, not moving a muscle, holding my breath. But I can't hear anything. Nothing at all. No voices. No footsteps in the alleyway behind the house. No car engine drifting into the distance on the way back to the barracks. Only the hoarse creaking of the door hinges in the yard and the huge lock turning and the distant toll of the bells ringing out two o'clock, stripped bare by the *cierzo*. But I wait another hour or so before I climb out of my hole. The darkness was so thick under the hay that now I can easily find my way around in the gloom of the hayloft.

A warm, pungent steam rises from the passage to the stables, a strong smell of old hay and manure, which, for some reason, suddenly rekindles far-off memories: playing with my sister in the hidden corners of the stable and, through the mists of time, a fair-haired boy carrying a saucepan of milk straight from the cow.

The yard is drenched with moonlight. I take a careful look around before crossing it. Bruna, the dog, jumps out of the shadows and comes towards me slowly, growling menacingly with bared teeth. She doesn't recognize me at first – she's almost blind, and I haven't been home for more than a year – but when she does she runs towards me and scrabbles against my chest, jumping for joy. But she doesn't bark. Perhaps she senses the danger from my silence. She follows me to the door and waits there calmly without a sound, on guard.

A distant glimmer in her near-blind eyes tells me that she is ready to defend my life with her own. Poor Bruna.

*

My father is sitting on the bed, under the blankets, propped up against the iron bars of the bedstead. He gives me an inscrutable look.

'What happened, Father?'

'What are you doing here?' he replies, not answering my question.

'I've come to see you. How are you?'

But my father hasn't even heard me. He gets off the bed and crosses the room. He rummages in a trunk and takes out a thin bundle of banknotes from among the clothes.

'What's this?' I say, trying to refuse it. It must be everything he has, all the money he's managed to scrape together in his long working life.

'Take it and don't say a word,' he insists in a dry voice, as if I were still a child and he was giving me this money to run an errand for him in Cereceda. 'Listen to me carefully, Ángel. You've got to get away from here, as far as possible, as soon as you can. Cross over to the other side if you can. They're out looking for you. No, they don't know you're here,' he says, reading the look of shock on my face. 'They're looking for everyone who was in Asturias. They know that a lot of you have come back across the mountains, and in the past few days they've caught quite a few. Benito the cartwright, Goro and two or three others from Ancebos. They're watching all the roads and villages.'

At the back of the room a streak of frozen silver pierces through the crack in the window shutter. It travels across the darkness, faintly illuminating my father's face. He's thin, very thin, and he's showing his age. There is a film of impotence mixed with rage in his eyes as he tries to contain his anger behind gritted teeth.

'You remember the mine on Mount Yormas, don't you? Where we sheltered from the rain years ago when we were out gathering firewood. Hole up there for the time being. See what happens. Juana or I will leave you some food on the hillside every three or four days.' And then, looking me straight in the eye, he says, 'But don't give yourselves up. Whatever happens, don't give yourselves up. Do you hear me? They'll kill you the next day and leave you in a ditch by the side of the road like they've done with so many others.'

'What happened at the barracks?' I ask him again from the doorway.

'Nothing.'

My father watches me leave, motionless in the shadows, his eyes impaled by the shaft of frozen silver that filters through the shutter.

*

Behind me, as I make my way up the mountain along the drovers' path, the clock-tower in La Llánava grinds out four slow peals. Four peals of wounded iron that explode into the night, showering my heart with something bitter, cold and mineral.

3

The light slashes the immense darkness of the earth's entrails like a bloody knife. The torch beam mingles with the cold black water flowing down from the ceiling and the walls, finally disappearing into a ghostly landscape of rusty rails, rotten timbers and a multitude of mysterious shafts and side-tunnels peeling off to the left and right of the main gallery.

The heat is humid and asphyxiating, fermenting like an animal's rotting corpse. It stinks. It impregnates the timbers and the water, the air and the silence with its penetrating stench.

Then it drifts along the gallery searching for an exit that isn't there.

*

'It's like we're dead. As if there's nothing else apart from this.' Ramiro, motionless until now, turns to look at me. He's stretched out on the board that he brought down from the minehead last night in order to protect himself from the water that runs non-stop through the gallery. That's how he spends his days, stock-still, silent, staring vacantly at the dilapidated beams that criss-cross the ceiling. 'You'll get used to it,' he says. 'People can get used to anything.'

'Except being buried alive.'

'Look at those two.'

Gildo and Juan are asleep near by, wrapped up in their capes, two black bundles in the darkness. Gildo's head is leaning against a lump of timber and his submachine-gun is strung across his body. His heavy build is striking in contrast to the slender, scrawny, almost childlike figure of Ramiro's brother, his adolescence still incomplete but already tainted with violence. Juan is not yet eighteen, and Gildo is over thirty. They could almost be father and son, although for now they are sleeping shoulder to shoulder, menaced by the same fear.

'In the mine at Ferreras they had mules to pull the carts,' says Ramiro, now staring vacantly at the tunnel ceiling again. 'They were born down there and they died down there. Their stables were on the first level, and they never went up to the surface. In one way that was for the best. That way they never got to know that they were blind and couldn't handle sunlight.'

'And we'll end up just like them if we stay down here too long,' I say.

Ramiro looks at me again with a strange smile on his face. A bitter smile, distant and expressionless. A smile that sweeps away the damp like it was dust. 'Do you know how many years I worked down the mine?' he asks. 'I'll tell you. Twelve. From the age of fifteen until I was twenty-seven, until the war broke out. And I didn't go blind.'

Gildo shifts his body, changes position under his cape and carries on sleeping, breathing noisily.

*

Ramiro and Gildo are going off to Gildo's house in Candamo to find some food, blankets and batteries for the torch, which petered

23

out definitively this morning, leaving us in darkness. Gildo still hasn't been to see his wife Lina and his son, who was born while he was in the trenches at Tejeda. He has been waiting impatiently for this moment ever since the night we arrived here.

Once they've gone, Juan and I eat a bit of bread, the last that remains of the two loaves my father brought up to the hillside for us the other night. We had to throw away the meat, which had gone bad because of the damp, so we have to make do with a bit of hard mouldy bread until Gildo and Ramiro get back from Candamo.

Then we stretch out again to count down the hours.

Now, up there, it must be getting dark. Maybe the sun is slowly retreating, pushed aside by the swollen November clouds. Maybe the wind is seeking consolation for its solitude among the heather and the oak trees. Maybe right now some shepherd is walking over the invisible hill above the mine.

Down here it is always night-time. There is no sun, no clouds, no wind, no horizons. Inside the mine, time doesn't exist. You lose your memory and your consciousness in an endless round of hours and days.

Inside the mine, there is only night-time.

*

The sun has gone, but the indestructible evening light beats violently against our eyes, which struggle to absorb so much light. So much light.

Out on the terrace, at the minehead, wooden boards, twisted iron rods, carts corroded by rust, rubble, all quietly rot in the evening chill, which is now retreating. The water suppurating from the depths of the mine spirals into a puddle of its own neglect, forming a dirty spring, a foul-smelling stream that trickles slowly through the heaps of rubble.

Inside the large shed, which must have once been the office and command centre, the only inhabitants now are solitude and neglect. There are scraps of slate and broken glass everywhere, and yellow weeds force their way up through the floorboards. It is as if some kind of plague had ravaged the whole place centuries ago.

In the distance, behind Mount Yormas, the sun dissolves into a dirty puddle.

*

When you forget the colour and texture of light, when the moon becomes your sun and the sun becomes a memory, your vision is guided more by scent than shapes, and your eyes follow the wind rather than seeking their own direction.

When the night wraps around everything, permanently and indefinitely, soaking the earth and the sky, annihilating feeling and time and memory, only instinct can find the right paths, guide you through the shadows and decipher the language of scent and sound.

*

The wind comes down to the valley at night to nestle in the stone quarries at Ancebos, under the red yew trees, locking the villagers and their dogs inside their houses next to the hearth. But now the wind is here as well. It beats against the dry branches, scratches furiously at the clay and disappears up the mountain with an endless black howl.

'We're nearly there. It's up there, behind the crag.' Gildo has stopped to wait for us. He points towards the enormous grey mass of Peña Barga sloping up in front of us, balanced precariously over the valley, abandoned in the night like an imaginary ship, like a boat stranded by the low tide. 'When we retreated to the north', says Gildo, panting from the effort, 'we went through there, through the pass. Can you see it? The sheepfold is just the other side.'

Gildo was on the front line here for nine days, the first nine days of the war. Gildo, like me, like Juan, like Ramiro, just like so many other men and women from these villages, had run for the hills by night when the area was split into two fronts divided by the railway line. He held out here for nine days. You can still see the trenches and the unexploded bombs and bits of shrapnel. Scars of a battle only Gildo can now remember.

'There were eight of us. Three from Ancebos, two from Vega-vieja, a miner from Ferreras, the blacksmith from La Moraña and me. I was the only one who survived. The other lot were in Ancebos. A whole section. We only had one machine-gun, but they lost loads of men getting past us.'

The wind sweeps through the pass. It's a stiff wind, and it makes our capes flap like the sad flags of a defeated army. The wind sweeps through the pass, dragging Gildo's memories down deep into the night's icy well.

*

There it is at last, on the other side of the rock, in the field that curves over the valley under a greeny-black deluge of broom.

There it is, gleaming under the moon, with its boundary wall of mud bricks, its roof eaten away by the snow. There is the stone shelter that protects the flock as they sleep and where the mastiffs have already scented our presence.

'Don't move! Drop the shotgun!'

The shepherd comes out of the shelter, alerted by the dogs. He comes out with the shotgun, perhaps thinking that some wild animal is loitering around the sheepfold or that the wolves have come down the mountain this far, pushed on by the snow in the passes, and that now they are waiting on the rock for the flock to go to sleep.

Instead, what he finds in front of his nose is Ramiro's handgun.

'I said drop the shotgun. Are you deaf or something?' The shepherd obeys. He throws the weapon to the ground, out of reach, and stands there looking at us with his hands in the air. 'Inside!'

A paraffin lamp, hanging from a beam in the ceiling, throws a milky light across the small room. There are logs piled up next to the fire and salt balls, jugs of milk, uncured animal skins, an old ramshackle bench, some sacks stacked untidily against the walls and a rickety old wooden bed on which the blankets betray the shepherd's interrupted sleep. At the back, strung across one corner halfway up the wall alongside spongy clouds of wool, is a wooden pail used to catch the yellow liquid dripping from the cheeses.

'It's just you here, right?'

The shepherd nods his head without taking his eyes off our submachine-guns. He's old, his face ravaged by that strange mixture of weariness and strength that the mountains always endow those who live there.

'OK,' says Ramiro, closing the door, 'in that case you're going to have company tonight. It's very cold out there.'

*

At five in the morning Gildo wakes me. I'd fallen asleep sitting in a corner.

I look around. Juan is also stretching, getting up from the bench and, at the back of the room, Ramiro is smoking quietly, watching the shepherd from the door. It's hot in here, surrounded by the sacks.

'What time is it?'

'Five o'clock.'

Gildo is putting a few cheeses away in a bag. He also takes a blanket and three or four uncured animal skins, under the impotent gaze of the shepherd, who is still sitting on the rickety bed. I recall that before I fell asleep he mentioned that a patrol of soldiers had come past that morning at dawn on their way to Tejeda, where they had set up a search team in the schoolhouse in order to comb the mountains. A patrol that could come back again at any time.

Ramiro stubs out his cigarette with his boot. 'We'll take one of the sheep', he says to the shepherd, 'and the shotgun. You'll get hold of another one easily enough.'

The man does not reply. He knows that he can't do anything to stop us. He gets up and leads the way to the shelter where the flock is sleeping under the watchful eyes of the faithful mastiffs.

The night is dying, and now the cold is much more intense, more cutting. It carries the fog's frosty lament on the edge of its tongue. The shepherd has gone in among the sheep. He looks at the scissor marks on their ears and, eventually, chooses one. He drags it towards us on a rope.

'Whose is it?'

The man looks at Ramiro in surprise. He hesitates for a moment then says, 'It's one of mine.'

Now it's Ramiro's turn to look surprised. 'Yours? Why one of yours?'

'If I give you someone else's, the *guardias* will find out sooner or later.'

Ramiro flashes him a sceptical grin. 'I thought you'd have told them yourself.'

The shepherd doesn't reply. He just shrugs his shoulders as he hands Juan the end of the rope so he can take charge of the sheep. The animal refuses to move. It struggles, with its hooves planted in the soil, trying to get back to the flock. Perhaps it has already read its fate in our eyes.

'Is that enough?'

It must have been the last thing the shepherd expected me to do at that moment. Ramiro and Gildo also look at me in astonishment. They didn't know about the money I've just taken out of my pocket. It's considerably more than double what it should be. Much more than the sheep and the shotgun and the few meagre things Gildo has in his bag are worth. It's considerably more than double, and the shepherd knows it. That's why he's still looking at me, bewildered, undecided whether or not to take the money I'm offering him.

'Here, take it. We pay our way, too,' I say. 'I hope what you said is true. Don't forget, we can always come back and pay you a visit one night.'

The shepherd watches us leave, standing at the door, surrounded by his mastiffs. It's almost certain that as soon as we disappear along the pass he'll go running down to the village to report what has happened to the *guardias*.

*

Dawn takes us by surprise back near the mine again. In one hour we've covered more than ten kilometres across the mountain.

There is a hard frost, as hard as glass, and huge low clouds drift across the sky filling the horizon and the mountains with dark light. Soon, for sure, once the cold dissolves with the frost, it will start to rain.

'Slow down, don't rush,' Gildo shouts. 'Wait for the lad.'

Juan comes up through the broom, tugging at the sheep.

'We need to kill it now', says Ramiro, 'before the sun comes up properly.'

'Where?'

'In the shed.'

'What about the entrails?'

'We'll throw them in the stream. It'll wash them down to where the water drains off the slagheaps.'

On the other side of the hill, under the skirts of Mount Yormas, we can just glimpse the terrace by the minehead: the shed's dilapidated panels, the empty water-tanks for the coal washery and the carts, eaten away by rust and frost. The wind beats gently against the grey slagheaps, which feed the hawthorn, sorrel and thistles.

It's a grey, futile, desolate landscape. A landscape abandoned to the remorseless voraciousness of time and oblivion.

Juan has caught up with us now, still dragging the sheep along. It walks behind him, docile and resigned, with the image of death etched on its face.

*

'Grab hold of it! Hang on tight! Tie its legs together! Quick!' Gildo struggles with the sheep, trying to force it to the ground. Finally, he succeeds. He holds it still by sticking his knee in its stomach, and I seize the moment to tie its legs together with the rope.

Ramiro and Juan watch us, at the same time keeping a lookout from the windows.

A few seconds later Gildo plunges his knife into the animal's throat. It thrashes on the ground, letting out a piercing scream. It convulses violently as the blood spurts impetuously from its gaping throat like wine out of a broken bottle. The blood spreads over the sheep's wool and the floorboards, among the rubble and broken glass. It splatters our shirts and gets in our eyes.

Gradually, the convulsions slow down and get weaker. Then all that remain are the death throes, the final spasms announcing that the end has arrived.

'Let go, Ángel. This one's not going anywhere now.' Gildo cleans the blade of his knife on his trousers, contemplating the sheep with an air of achievement. It is stretched out on the ground, in the middle of a huge puddle of blood. 'Now we have to skin it,' he says, lifting it up by the back legs. 'Help me hang it from this beam.'

The light creeping through the windows of the shed is progressively sharper, more clear and transparent. It's dawn already, and a weak winter sun is trying to break out on the other side of the hill. For now it is still just a yellow stain watered down by the clouds.

'Hold its head. Don't let it tip over.'

The sheep hangs from the beam like a strange, bloody fruit, and the knife moves purposefully down through its stomach, releasing a torrent of entrails over the broken rusty cauldron that Ramiro found in the washery. Gildo folds up his sleeves and plunges one arm inside the animal's body. He pulls out foul-smelling handfuls

31

of innards with rapid, expert movements. The scraps slop against the bottom of the cauldron with a dull grey sound.

Gildo's arm is streaked with blood, like ivy on a tree trunk.

'Juan, throw this into the stream and bring me some fresh water. Quickly.' Juan carries the cauldron out of the shed, and Gildo, cleaning his knife again, starts to peel off the animal's skin. 'It's a good one,' he says. 'It would make a good jacket –'

But he doesn't have time to finish. Juan bursts into the shed and runs towards one of the windows. 'There's someone up there! He's seen me!'

Ramiro, Gildo and I run up to join him.

'Are you sure?'

'Of course I'm sure. Look up there at the top of the hill.'

Ramiro looks through his binoculars at the silhouette outlined against the horizon. 'It's a boy,' he says.

'What's he doing up there?'

'How should I know?'

Ramiro scans the whole hillside opposite us, looking for any others. Then he looks back to where he started from. 'He's coming down towards us,' he says. 'He's on his own.'

Two minutes later the boy is standing next to the terrace.

Now we can see him clearly. He must be fourteen or fifteen, just a bit younger than Juan. He's carrying a rope and seems to be looking for something. He's standing still in the field of broom, near the washery, and he's looking at the shed with curiosity and suspicion, perhaps not daring to come any closer.

'He's seen us. He must have.'

'Ángel, you go out and get him away from here,' Ramiro says, squatting beside me under the window. 'But don't make him suspicious.'

I leave the submachine-gun on the floor, clean the blood off my hands with a rag and walk slowly to the door.

On the terrace I'm struck by the frozen light of daybreak.

The boy looks at me, motionless in the middle of the broom. He hesitates before asking me, 'Hey there! Have you seen a goat around here?'

I pretend that I've just noticed him. 'No, I haven't seen a thing. Has it gone missing?'

'Yes. She didn't come back with the rest of the herd last night.'

'Where are you from?'

'Vegavieja.' The boy seems to trust me because he has left his position in the broom and started to walk towards the terrace. If I don't do something to stop him he'll get to the shed. 'She's stayed out on the mountain before,' he says, 'but now she's pregnant, and my father's scared that she'll hide out up there to give birth on her own, and she could be carried off by the wolves or trapped by a snowfall…'

Suddenly, his eyes fall on the cauldron full of bloody entrails that Juan has left next to the sluice. He backs away. Then he starts to run up the hillside through the broom without giving me time to react. He looks around every so often to make sure that I'm not following him.

Once he's near the top of the hill, he shouts down to me, threatening and frightened at the same time. 'It was you! You stole her!'

Then he runs off and disappears into the clouds.

'Let's get out of here,' says Ramiro, coming out on to the terrace. 'Before the hour's up this place will be crawling with soldiers.'

*

Around about midday the clouds burst. They could no longer bear the silence.

First of all they softened like ripened fruits, then they crashed into each other and finally their swollen bellies split open, spewing out a bitter black substance over the ground.

Lower down the mountainside, the clusters of broom bowed their heads submissively as the rain passed over.

*

'There they are.'

We are lying face down on the crest of the hillock that crowns the vertical summit of Mount Yormas like a broken cockerel's comb. From this vantage point, with the help of the binoculars, we can take in a much more grandiose and beautiful landscape than we could with the naked eye: the weightless mass of the Peña Negra, the green chasm of the Los Osos Valley and the passes at La Friera and Vegavieja, the broken needles of Mount Usiello, behind Peña Barga; towards the west the Tejeda and La Moraña passes, Mount Morana, the snowy peaks of the Sierra de la Sangre where Lake Negro and the River Susarón have their sources; the silvery and familiar outline of Mount Illarga, faded by the rain and the distance. And, down below us, under our noses, like the tiny eruptions of a cursed and forgotten land, the grey slagheaps from the mine and the edge of the slope bordering the south end of the terrace, now broken by the silhouettes of men who are moving forward, fanned out, weapons at the ready, like a huge hunting party.

'Just as well we got out of that death trap in time.' It's Ramiro's voice. He's pressed flat against the crest of the rock beside me, almost hanging over the void.

The wind howls like a wolf, scattering the rain in every direction. The clouds are so low that they are almost leaning in on us.

*

Spread out at the edge of the terrace, in the broom, the *guardias* and the soldiers have surrounded the slag heaps and have taken up positions around the water-tanks and the shed.

They spend a few minutes observing the mine works, in the rain, and then a voice shouts out from the broom, 'Come out with your hands in the air. There's no way out.'

But the only reply from inside the shed is an eerie silence.

Finally, after another pause, several *guardias* jump out of the broom and run across the terrace and jump behind the wagons and the water-tanks. Some of them reach the drainage ditch and throw themselves down in the mud just twenty metres away from the shed.

Now, down there, you can hear unintelligible voices, shouts muffled by the downpour. One *guardia* has left his temporary position behind a wagon and is running on his own, stooped over, towards the shed, covered by rapid fire from his colleagues who are still lying in the ditch. He flattens himself against the wall, next to the door, and looks nervously towards the broom, waiting for orders. The silence is so tense that even the rain has gone quiet in anticipation of the dénouement.

A few interminable seconds go by before the *guardia* makes his decision. He kicks the door open and aims his weapon at the empty room.

'Our gallant heroes will just have to wait,' Ramiro mutters with a smile.

But then I notice something moving on the terrace. Everyone

35

has now left their hiding places in the broom, and several *guardias* are going towards the entrance to the mine, their guns pointing at two men in handcuffs. They make them go in first so that they act as a shield in case someone opens fire from inside.

The rest of the *guardias* and the soldiers wait outside on the terrace, sniffing around the shed and the washery.

They don't have to wait long, however. After a few minutes, two gunshots rip through the belly of the mountain. It's a deep, rumbling sound, like dynamite exploding underground. For a moment it disrupts the perfect equilibrium of the silence and the rain.

When the party regroups on the terrace and starts to move off again towards Tejeda, the two prisoners are no longer part of it.

4

The meat crackles on the fire at the back of the cave while, outside, the November wind blows leaves from far away across the mountains.

There is dense, acrid smoke pervading the passageway that accumulates against the cape stretched over the mouth of the cave to stop the glow of the fire from being seen from outside. After a whole day enduring the damp and the cold that suppurate out from the bowels of the earth it's good to smell the pungent aroma of the roast meat and listen to the monotonous crackling of the flames, their oaky tongues licking the meat as it shrinks with a slow lament.

'Good. It's ready.' Gildo has plunged his knife into the shrunken, quivering chunk of meat and taken it off the fire in order to dice it up on a flat rock.

We watch him without interest. Juan is stretched out on a couple of blankets at some distance from the fire, and Ramiro, opposite me, is leaning against the dark wall of the passageway, half asleep in the grip of a deep tedium. His position and expression have hardly changed all day. Or, rather, his position and expression have hardly changed since we've been buried down here in this damp hole. Tomorrow it will be a whole week. It was just a hollow, choked up with mud and broom, which at one time must have been a shepherd's refuge. When we arrived here after fleeing from the abandoned mine we spent five long nights of hard labour in the pitch black, digging it out and making it larger with only a knife and a spade for tools. Despite the protection of the wooden boards, which we brought up from the old shed at the mine to line the ceiling and walls, the cave is damp and freezing cold, only fit for wild animals. But it is completely hidden behind the thick fronds of broom, hanging off the sheer crest of the Peña Illarga like an eagle's nest, and no one, not even the oldest shepherds from the local villages, would still remember it. Best of all, we can look out with our binoculars from the narrow mouth of the cave's entrance over the entire valley along the River Susarón, with its two villages, Pontedo and La Llánava, and the road that comes down from Ferreras, the black railway line and the ashen walls of the Cereceda Barracks.

'What's up with you?' asks Gildo. 'Aren't you going to eat anything?'

The response is an indifferent silence. Ramiro and Juan don't even open their eyes to look at him.

I'm not hungry either. Since we got here I've scarcely felt the terrible moaning of the beast in the depths of my stomach, which bayed despairingly so many times in the final months of the war. It was even worse during the five days when we did not eat at all as we fled across the mountains, in the rain, from a more physical beast, more human and bloodthirsty, which pursued us implacably. It is as if the dampness and cold of the cave have penetrated my bones and my soul, imprisoning me here, lying beside the fire day and night with no interest in eating or talking or even peering through the mouth of the cave to look at the hard, overcast sky. Its edges are already tinged with the promise of snow, and we all know what that means. We will not be able to escape from here until the spring.

'Well, it's up to you,' says Gildo, brandishing a piece of roast meat on his knife, 'but remember, this is all we have left.'

He starts eating voraciously, letting the fat run over his hands, swollen by the cold, and over his thick, heavy beard.

*

Around three in the morning an owl is hooting in the hollow of some nearby oak tree. It will be red and black, like the campfire, which is dying back in the cave, and its eyes will be shining in the night like two bright coals.

*

When I wake up, the freezing, flickering light of dawn is already filtering in through the mouth of the cave. The fire has gone out, burned down to the embers, and the damp has gone right through my blanket and cape.

'Are you awake?' It's Ramiro. I can see his eyes shining in front of me in the darkness, and I'm reminded of the owl hooting in the night.

'Yes. What time is it?'

'Seven o'clock. It's daybreak.'

I lie back awkwardly on the heap of woollens and leaves I have been sleeping on. My hands are hard, swollen by the cold, with barely the strength to hold the bottle Ramiro offers me in the darkness.

'Here, have a drink. It will help you fight off the cold.'

I lean back against the icy rock and pull out the cork. The

brandy burns a fiery strip at the back of my throat. The brandy is like an iron river exploding furiously against the vaults of sleep, searching my memory for the painful recollection of the night. The bitter flame of its breath is the only flame we are allowed during daylight on the mountain, when the smoke from a fire can be seen from the valley.

'There's movement down there,' says Ramiro, watching me drink. His voice is almost a whisper. There is a strange glint in his eyes, an inscrutable, fleeting brilliance that always appears when there is danger about.

'What's happening?'

'I don't know. But two truckloads of reinforcements have arrived.'

'When?'

'First thing this morning. Come and see.'

I leave the bottle on the floor, on the blankets, and crawl after Ramiro to the mouth of the cave.

The Cereceda Valley opens up at the foot of the rock like an inverted sky, like a huge cooking pot from which a thick, freezing vapour rises up towards us. The fog is so dense, so curdled, that it is now impossible to discern the outline of the woods or the shape of the mountains. Everything slowly melts into the same colour and into one mass, a grey, worn-out layer, torn only by the needle-like tops of the poplar trees next to the river and by the red rooftops of Pontedo and La Llánava.

'Can you see anything?'

Ramiro tries and fails to see anything through the fog with his binoculars. 'Nothing. The fog's coming up very fast. A moment ago you could clearly see the barracks and the two trucks in the yard.'

Suddenly, almost at the same time, both of us are gripped by the same doubt. I can read it in Ramiro's eyes, wide open and ablaze, just as he is probably reading the same thing in mine. The trucks must still be there in the fog-bound barracks. But what about the *guardias* who arrived in them?

Ramiro runs back down the passage to get his brother and Gildo. They wake up with a start, wrapped in their blankets, next to the remains of the fire. They still don't understand why we are so agitated. But without wasting time, they grab their submachine-guns and follow us.

*

Outside, in the broom, the fog is like a sheet of tight, shimmering gauze. It shuts off the light and blurs the lines of the bushes, which open a path for us, rustling as we pass.

I watch Ramiro's boots crunching over the grass as we head towards the upper slopes, climbing the side of the rock just in front of my eyes and the steamy breath from my mouth. I can hear Juan's footsteps behind me, close on my heels, and I can imagine Gildo's boots bringing up the rear through the lingering fog. We can't see a thing. No sound reaches us announcing a distant battle, but we all know that the presence of those two trucks down there is a portent of death and uncertainty. And that this is the time, daybreak, when the scant light still permits a stealthy advance through the heather, and sleep can sometimes cause a fugitive to lower his guard. This is the time the *guardias* always choose to come up the mountain in pursuit.

High up on the rock we lie flat on the ground, buried in the heather, back to back. The fog envelops us with a silent roar.

The fog into which the *guardias*' breath might already be melting near by.

*

It's a false alarm. Another one. One of so many. When the fog draws back we return to the cave. The trucks leave in the afternoon.

*

None of us can talk him out of it. Not even Ramiro. Juan's the only one who's never been down the mountain.

'Mother's waiting for me. I'll bring back some food and blankets.'

'I'll go down with you.'

'No, I'm going down on my own. You've all been down a few times. Tonight it's my turn to take the risk.' Juan picks up his submachine-gun and his brother's handgun. He stuffs a handful of cartridges into his pocket and goes off through the heather towards La Llánava.

We watch him go until he disappears over the crest of the hill.

*

'Ángel.' It's Ramiro. Again.

'What?'

'Are you asleep?'

'I'm not tired.'

'What time do you think it is?'

'I don't know. Two o'clock? Half past two?'

'He's been gone a very long time, don't you think?' Ramiro sits back in silence, staring at the fire. Staring at the fire and waiting for a reply from me. But I don't have one.

Towards daybreak the wind comes up. It whips around the

cape stretched over the mouth of the cave, peeps its transparent head inside to take a look at us and then goes away again down the mountain.

Juan has still not come back.

Ramiro returns from the broom field and puts out the fire. 'It's daybreak,' he says.

Gildo and I look at him in silence.

'Something's happened to Juan.'

For a while now I've been greasing up my submachine-gun, trying to calm my nerves.

'Something's happened to my brother,' Ramiro shouts suddenly, completely unhinged. 'Don't just sit there!'

Gildo looks at me. He doesn't know what to do, or, rather, he knows, like me, that the only thing we can do is stay here. Sit and wait until nightfall.

*

Throughout the day we take turns to scan the valley through the binoculars: the thicket covering the hillsides, the paths, the riverbanks, the streets in La Llánava, the black single-track railway.

Nothing. Not a trace of Juan. Not the slightest sign of his presence.

In the barracks the normal rhythm of patrols and pounding the beat seems to rule out any extraordinary event.

*

The mill looms up, expressionless and cheerless, beside the race where the mill wheels are sleeping with their teeth sunk into the water. The noise of the water in the weir is torrential. But a deep, domestic, wintry calm gently envelops the leafless poplars lining the road.

A light is shining through the window of the mill, a yellow coagulation that sprinkles over the foam in the mill race and the willows on the riverbank.

Tomás, the miller, is alone in the kitchen. I can see his washed-out face through the window. He's propped up on his elbows, sitting at the table with the remains of his supper, his back to the fire. It's eleven o'clock at night, and Tomás, who lives here on his own, separated from the village by the river, is killing time, listening to the news on the radio before he goes to bed. The cold night and the fear of an encounter on the road make a visit to the village bar somewhat unappealing.

But today Tomás has a visitor. At this time of night? Surely not. Tomás listens attentively. He turns down the volume on the radio. Now he can hear it. Now he can hear it clear as day: a gentle knock on the window, muffled by the frost.

The miller stands up and goes to the window very slowly. Suspicious, he studies the night's shadows through the window panes.

When he sees me and recognizes me, the surprise petrifies him.

*

'On the mountain?'

'For the past month. You probably think we're mad.'

Tomás has shot the bolt across the door and closed the shutters on the window. And he's turned off the radio.

He doesn't know that Gildo is outside, keeping watch.

'What I think is mad', he says, 'is you coming here. You're

taking a big risk yourselves and you're also dragging me into it.'

'I know, Tomás, and I'm sorry, I really am. But we need your help. That's why we've come to see you.'

Ramiro listens silently by the door. The miller doesn't know who to look at, Ramiro or me. He probably thinks that we are going to ask if he can hide us at the mill, and it is pretty obvious that he doesn't much like the idea. He knows how risky that would be for him.

'What do you want?'

'We're looking for my brother,' says Ramiro, breaking the silence at last. 'He's with us on the mountain. Last night he came down to our house to get blankets and food, and he still hasn't come back.'

'So you want me to go to your house to find out what's happened?'

'Exactly,' says Ramiro. 'It's too risky for us. If they've caught my brother the *guardias* will have the whole village under surveillance.'

'If they'd caught him we'd know already,' says Tomás, perhaps in an attempt to calm our fears or to give himself an excuse. 'Your brother must be hiding somewhere in the house.'

Ramiro and I look at him without saying a word. The miller, standing in front of us, dead still, seems more and more indecisive. He's obviously scared to go out on his own and go down to La Llánava on this strange night, full of fears and omens. On this strange night, shot through with an icy chill.

But he can't find the courage to refuse us the help we ask of him. 'You wait for me here,' he says finally, looking at the clock and reaching for his sheepskin jacket. 'I'll be back soon.'

*

45

The church clock is chiming midnight when we see him coming back down the road. It's only been half an hour. Ramiro and I have joined Gildo by the fence alongside the mill race, since neither of us could stand the anxious wait in the darkness of the kitchen. We see Tomás coming towards us with his hands sunk deep in the pockets of his sheepskin jacket and his body leaning forward into the wind.

He jumps when he sees us appear at the side of the road. 'He's not there', he says, looking at Ramiro. 'And he wasn't there last night either.'

'He wasn't there last night?'

The miller hesitates for a moment, then he says, 'That's right. Unless your mother's lying.'

A frozen gust of wind has clipped his last sentence. Suddenly, the water in the mill race falls silent behind the weir. The sky turns the colour of rusty iron and, through the tops of the poplar trees, the moon is sinking like a rotten fruit.

It's the sign. Suddenly, it starts snowing gently on the desolate fields, on the endless expanses of the night, on the eternal lonely places by the river and the road.

*

As we go past the last of the orchards, nearly at the cemetery, the snowstorm really sets in. It comes howling down the mountain, bending the trees double like sacrificial lambs bowing before some passing god.

In just a few minutes, the time it's taken us to get from the mill to here on the hillside, the snow has started to stick on the road. It's a dirt road, fenced on either side, crossing through the orchards and the fields along the riverbanks. It makes its way lazily up the hill to the cemetery and then it becomes a twisting drovers' path, climbing up the mountain.

Just here, as we break into the open mountain, they hit us point blank with the volley, a curtain of fire that suddenly bursts out of the crumbling cemetery walls.

Once I get my bearings back I'm lying face down in the middle of the path. Blinded by the snow, feeling the steely tongues of the bullets all around me, I run for the shelter of the heather. Gildo is already there, gripping his submachine-gun furiously and with intent.

'Let them have it', Ramiro screams behind me, 'before they cut us to pieces!'

The night has exploded like a barrel of gunpowder. It's turned into a devastating, freezing tornado. The snow, the wind, the rattle of gunfire, the shouts of the *guardias*, all fuse together in the night creating a blurred, inscrutable backdrop. The noise is out of this world. Everywhere we turn bullets seek out our bodies, ricocheting off the ground in an endless howl.

'We've got to get out of here,' Gildo shouts beside me, still firing his weapon. 'We've got to get out of here!'

'Hold on! Hold on!' Pressed flat against the road, Ramiro reaches into his belt for a hand-grenade. He pulls out the pin with his teeth and throws it with all his strength towards the invisible shadows of the *guardias*.

The roar of the explosion is deafening. For a few seconds, there is not a sound of the *guardias*' voices or the rattle of their weapons. We run desperately up the mountain into the night and the snowstorm.

'Let them have it! Let's go, cover me!'

Ramiro has another grenade in his fist and, before the *guardias* can react, a second explosion forces them down behind the orchard walls.

And here we go again, running, running up the mountain with all our strength, running through the heather and the snowy gusts, running in search of the deepest roots of the night, the safety of the rocks that, high up on the mountain, mark the border between life and death.

Suddenly, I feel something hit my knee.

'Wait for me!'

A dull thud, out of nowhere, and an intense burning sensation that runs up my leg like a flame.

'Wait! Wait for me! I've been hit!'

'Run! Don't stop! Keep running!'

I drop to the ground, into the undergrowth, and I drag myself along as best I can up to the rock. Gildo is up above already, firing his weapon.

Ramiro comes up beside me. 'Where have you been hit?'

'Here, my knee.'

The burning sensation gets stronger and stronger, more intense. I try to stop the warm flow of blood with my hand.

'Here. Strap it up with this scarf.' Ramiro grabs my submachine-gun and climbs up the rock to join Gildo. 'Hold your fire,' he says. 'They won't come up here.'

*

After a few minutes a short desperate machine-gun burst puts an end to the shoot-out.

The night is reluctant to yield to silence. It's too intense. But, instantaneously, the grey howl of the snowstorm resurfaces from somewhere in the heather and fills the vacuum left by the gunpowder. In the distance a few stray lights come on in the windows of La Llánava.

Gradually, the *guardias* start to emerge from behind the orchard wall. They approach the road cautiously and fearfully at first. Then they are convinced that by now we are over the other side of the hill, lost in the night, well out of range. There are only four of them. For a long while they do a torchlight search along the drovers' path, through the scrub and heather, along the edge of the rocks, right under our noses.

Ramiro was right. In the end, their torches pierce the sky, above the rocks, but they don't dare come up the mountain to look for us.

*

On the Illarga hillside, the snow is now ankle deep. The snowstorm has abated, and now the mountain is bathed in a cold, dense calm.

I'm leaning on Gildo's shoulder, sinking deeper into the snow with each step, with not a moment's rest, not even the briefest of pauses to look back and contemplate the long wake of silence we leave between us and the boots of the *guardias*. All I can feel is the bitter stinging that chews into my knee like an insect. The rocks get larger and larger before my eyes. The snowdrifts fuse with the heather and then unfuse, dull and insensitive, against my hands and my face.

I think I'm going to faint. I feel a deep black lake burst in my brain. 'Stop,' I plead. 'I can't go on.'

Gildo stops and lets me flop on to the snow. He pulls off the bloody scarf so he can look at my wound. 'Let's go, Ángel. Grit your teeth. It's not far now.' Gildo cleans the scarf in the snow

49

and ties it tightly around my knee. The wet scarf stops the insect's stinging, but, in exchange, a sharp pain cuts across my back like a whiplash.

Ramiro uses a branch to rub out the trail of blood I've left in the snow. 'OK to go?' he asks.

'Yes,' I say, not knowing if I can even get to my feet.

And I can't. By now I can't feel any of my limbs. Between the two of them they get me up. Gildo lifts me across his shoulders and starts walking, clumsily.

*

Almost at the cave, Gildo drops me down on to the snow again and picks up his submachine-gun.

Ramiro moves forward. He goes into the broom and checks all the security markers with his torch, the barely perceptible markers (a broken branch, a tin can, a bit of string) that we always leave at the entrance to the cave to check whether someone has been here in our absence.

'Juan?' Ramiro's voice rips through the rock's frozen entrails like a knife. 'Juan? Are you there?'

But no one replies.

Part Two
1939

Part Two
1935

5

The bus from León to Ferreras passes through Casasola every day at seven in the morning, regular as clockwork. It stops briefly in front of the church (where the porch is used as an improvised shelter on rainy days and in the winter), crosses the stone bridge over the river and, with its headlights still blazing, starts to climb lazily up the lower slopes of the Fresnedo Pass.

Today is market day in León, and the bus is packed with farmers, who have all got up very early to feed the animals and have a shave. So it is more of a struggle to get up the hills than usual. Occasionally the road flattens out allowing the bus a breather, but on the slopes it splutters like an old metallic ox on the brink of collapse.

Now it has crossed the green line of poplars that runs alongside the river. It pauses as if to gather breath, sighs and launches itself weakly uphill in pursuit of the next bend. And so on until it approaches the top of the pass. Just like every other day.

Ramiro pulls his balaclava down over his face and takes out his handgun.

'Ready?'

Gildo and I both nod back to him. We release the safety catches on our submachine-guns and lie flat in the brambles by the side of the road.

The bus is going into the last bend in the road. Its dusty grey snout squeezes against the rock face at the side of the road, snatching at the thicket that is growing there. Suddenly, it whinnies, like a horse when someone tugs sharply at the reins. Its tyres struggle for purchase on the road. The bus pauses for a moment then lets out a long deep sigh and finally stops, exhausted, next to the tree trunk that has been straddling the road, lying in wait, since the bus set off from Casasola.

That's when we all jump out from the side of the road.

'Everyone stay calm. Stay in your seats.' Before the passengers realize what's happening, Ramiro is inside the bus, shouting. 'Everyone off the bus and line up against the rock! Hands up!' He turns to the bus driver and says, 'You first.'

The passengers obey quickly and without saying a word. Like a flock of startled sheep, they get off the bus and line up against the rock. One or two of them look at us suspiciously, trying to make out who we are, but faced with our balaclavas and the threat of the submachine-guns they soon give up.

Ramiro gets off last. He puts his gun back in its holster and starts frisking the passengers one by one. He puts the money in his pocket and throws the wallets to the side of the road, in a heap. The passengers let him search them, resigned to their fate. Occasionally, Ramiro might skip over one of them. Maybe that man looks like he needs the money more than we do, or that young woman, clutching a child in her arms, has helped us on more than one occasion, but he makes sure that none of the other passengers realizes what he's doing.

The search only takes five minutes. When he's finished, Ramiro stands to one side. 'You can get back on the bus. Remember, keep your hands up.'

The passengers do as they are told, this time more quickly.

They go back to their seats without saying a word and without even daring to look out through the windows.

The last two drag the tree trunk to the side of the road, and it rolls a few metres down the slope.

'Let's go!'

The roar of the engine breaks the deep silence of the morning once again. The bus, its unscheduled breather now over, stretches out and slowly starts to climb the last bit of the slope and disappears around the bend, enveloped in a cloud of black smoke.

*

The blue-chequered pinafore dress is hanging in the garden in the branches of the cherry tree that my father planted next to the well the day my mother was buried so we would think of her every time summer returned to La Llánava.

The pinafore dress is dry. Juana or my father have hung it up there to let me know that the *guardias* are watching the house.

*

'Are they still there?' It's María's voice behind me.

'Yes.'

'Well then, go back to bed. Get some sleep.'

'I've spent the past two days sleeping. I've spent two days and two nights cooped up in here.'

'Well?' María's voice is thick and heavy. 'Aren't you better off here than out there on the mountain?'

The gap in the shutter lets in a shaft of moonlight, which cuts through the shadows and shines on the bed. My eyes slowly become used to the darkness, to the location of objects in the gloom: the wardrobe made of varnished walnut, the chest where

María keeps her clothes between sprigs of mint, the broken mirror where I leaned my submachine-gun.

María gently presses against me, from behind. 'You smell like the mountain,' she says. 'You smell like a wolf.'

'What else would I be?'

María turns around and looks at me. I feel the tremor of her body, hot and uncomfortable in her slip. The sharp tremor of a lonely woman, still young and pretty but condemned to wait for ever for a shadow, a ghost. Feeding her memories of a man who will never return. A woman who in recent years has fused her loneliness with mine on so many nights.

'You can't carry on like this, Ángel. You can't live like animals for ever. Worse than animals. They don't hunt animals the way they hunt you.'

'What else can we do? Put a bullet in our heads or hand ourselves in so they can save us the trouble?'

María looks at me in silence. She squeezes her stomach against mine and starts kissing me. I feel the blood rushing to my head in waves. I kiss her forcefully, almost angrily, as if I'd never kissed her before. As if the endless lonely nights, full of desire, in the depths of the cave had all surfaced at once. As if only now, and never again, would I be able to kiss her.

She slowly envelops my hips with her thighs, and stares deep into my eyes.

*

I am woken by the church bells, slow, monotonous and far away.

María, her arms still wrapped around me, turns over in her sleep. Her crumpled slip is scrunched up around her waist, and she carries on sleeping.

On the bedside table, next to my handgun and tobacco, the clock says five o'clock in the morning.

I get up without making a sound and creep towards the window. The moon dazzles my eyes, blinding me. But, almost immediately, it slips behind a cloud, tracing my father's garden against the sky, between the trees and the village rooftops.

Juana's chequered pinafore is not there any more.

*

The moon is nestling in María's walnut tree tonight. The moonlight scratches the shadows of the garden walls as I leave the house, in silence, slowly, cautiously, like when we were children and we used to search around here for forbidden fruit from the orchards or from the red lips of the young village girls.

The only difference is that now my submachine-gun leaves a shadow of death on the ground like an elongated ear of wheat.

*

Tonight, like every night, my father has left the back door that opens on to the alley unbarred.

I just have to go through the door and climb on to the woodshed, crawl over the bundles of oak and dried heather and, now inside, swing into the unlit barn in which the cart and the farming tools have always been stored. That's where Bruna the dog used to sleep until a *guardia* blew her head off with a bullet from his rifle.

Inside the house it is absolutely pitch black. The corridor stretches like a dark mouth to the foot of the stairs and the kitchen door, which I can just make out with the help of my cigarette lighter.

A creak on the stairs. A familiar voice. 'Ángel? Is that you?' My father is on the landing, still dressed.

'Yes, Father, it's me. Why are you still awake?'

He doesn't answer my question.

'Come upstairs', he says, 'quickly', and he disappears up the stairs without waiting for me.

*

I stand at the door, motionless, speechless, as if I had just been given an electric shock.

Under the yellow light of a candle I can see my sister's body stretched out feebly on the bed, with her head bent over a washbasin full of bloody water.

My father is sitting beside her. He helps her to sit up, to rest her head against the pillow.

Juana looks at me, her eyes brimming with tears. 'I'm OK now, Ángel. Don't worry. I'm feeling better now,' she says, her voice faltering. 'I've just been sick, that's all.'

As she lies there in silence, exhausted, thick red spittle oozes from her lips, and my father gently wipes it away with the edge of the sheet.

'They gave her a hiding. They took her into the stables, and they punched and kicked her black and blue.' My father, consumed by impotence and rage, looks like a broken tree against the yellow light of the candle. 'They wouldn't let me leave the kitchen. They wouldn't dare mess with me, you know? They wouldn't mess with me, those bastards.' Then, calming down, he adds, 'I'm worried, Ángel. She's been spitting blood.'

'Get a neighbour to go down to Cereceda and find a doctor. Don't you budge from here. You stay here with Juana.'

'He'll refuse to come, you'll see. Just like before. The doctor's even worse than the *guardias*.'

'Well, at least let him know. And also let him know that, one day, he might find me waiting for him.'

My father stands there, not saying a word, looking at my sister. He wipes her lips again with the sheet. I stay in the doorway, unable to find the words to console him. Not knowing how to tell him that I'm suffering more for them than for myself. Not knowing how to put a stop to this endless bloody cycle.

So I turn and leave without saying anything.

*

Gildo opens the can of meat with his knife. Behind his broad back, in the distance, I can see the outline of the mountains and the blood-red remains of a sunset.

He points, behind him, to the imposing peaks of Mount Morana. 'We could go up by the river.'

Ramiro chews on a piece of meat without much appetite. 'Where would we cross?' he asks. 'The river's swollen.'

'By the bridge.'

'Hangman's Bridge?'

'Of course.'

Ramiro shakes his head. 'You must be joking. It's a death trap. Just one *guardia*, hiding on the rock, could cut us to pieces. We'll go up by the Peña Negra. We're not in any hurry.'

Ramiro, as ever, is cautious. He analyses every move we make, leaving nothing to chance. Sometimes I find it hard to recognize the shy, quiet boy I played with so many times at school or the boy who looked after the herds with me on the pastures near La Llánava. I find it hard because now, here in front of me, all I can see is a remote, elusive man, a cornered beast who knows that sooner or later he'll end up being cut down by bullets on one of those mountainsides he is studying now with that inscrutable look of his.

'Keep the tin,' he says to Gildo. 'It might come in useful.'

Gildo puts the tin in his knapsack, and we set off again.

All three of us know there's only one thing that bit of tin might be useful for, once it's full of explosives and shrapnel.

*

On the Peña Negra the night is a sheet of stars and blueberries.

As we make our way, skirting around the edge of the rock, the vegetation disappears gradually under the scree that covers the hillside. We are leaving the valley further and further below. It sinks lower and lower into the sea of ferns and broom, which the River Susarón runs through noisily.

On the Peña Negra, there is nothing but blueberries. And stones. And solitude. And stars.

On the Peña Negra, there is nothing but three shadows walking silently into the wind.

*

La Llera, cradled beside the carved-out riverbed, is little more than a handful of houses and elm trees nestled together, like a flock of sheep, at the foot of the Peña Negra.

Just in front of the first houses there is a lush green field. It looks white under the moon and is draped down the hill, searching for fresh, cool water. Then, once down below, the field stretches out gently on both sides of the river, which goes off towards Vegavieja and the Valselada coal-washing plants.

La Llera has a ruined church, a mediaeval tower eaten away by time and wild lichen and a stone schoolhouse where I was teaching on the morning the war arrived here. I've not seen it since.

Now, however, I'm right beside it, hiding in its shadow with Gildo and Ramiro. Through the windows, gently lit up by the moon, I can see the rows of pupils' desks, the teacher's desk – my old desk – and the blackboard on the wall. Everything is just as I left it that summer's morning.

But Gildo and Ramiro don't have any memories here, and they wait impatiently, watching the house I've just pointed out to them.

'The door to the yard's unlocked,' says Gildo.

'Yes, but be careful. He's bound to have a gun.'

The door opens without a sound. The yard is shrouded in darkness and silence, but I can make out a reddish light at the back, framed in a window full of cobwebs.

Suddenly, a dog comes out to meet us. It has menacing eyes. But, before it has time to realize what's happening a choke knot tightens around its throat. The animal stares at us, tied to the cartwheel with its eyes stained with surprise and blood.

Through the stable window I can see the man we've come looking for. He's sitting on a stool milking a cow.

Gildo and Ramiro wait outside to cover my retreat.

*

The man turns around on his stool, still holding the pail, alerted by my footsteps. At first he just looks surprised, but when he sees that it's me the muscles in his neck and around his mouth snap taut and his face goes completely white. He looks at me incredulously, his eyes popping out of their sockets.

'What's up, Guillermo?' I say, standing in front of him in the middle of the stable. 'Don't you recognize me?'

He doesn't dare to respond.

'You look like you've seen a ghost.'

The milk pail falls between his legs, leaving a puddle of milk on the straw. The cows shuffle around, disconcerted.

'Or perhaps you thought I was dead.'

'No, no. Why do you say that?' He has spoken at last, in a low, startled voice. He sounds very different from the night he led the search for me as I lay hidden in a hayloft until I could get away to the mountains.

'Didn't you hear what happened to me?'

'Yes,' he says, in barely a whisper. 'I knew you'd escaped, to the hills.'

'And you never thought I might come and pay you a visit one day?'

He doesn't reply. He is paler beyond the limits of fear, and a cold sallow sweat runs down his face.

He stands up without taking his eyes off me.

'What are you going to do, Ángel? What are you going to do?'

I point the submachine-gun towards that feeble bulk, that blurred image. His eyes are begging me for mercy, but he can't find the words.

I wait a few seconds until the silence wells up into a cloud, before I burst it. 'Listen to me, Guillermo. I'm not going to kill you this time. Do you understand? I'm not going to kill you this time. But, right now, as soon as I've gone, you get on that horse of yours and go straight to Cereceda and pay a visit to the sergeant on my behalf. Tell him that this is just a warning. Because of what happened to my sister. He'll know what I mean. But tell him that next time, someone – you perhaps – will end up on the side of the road with a bullet in his head. Do I make myself clear, Guillermo? Do I make myself clear?'

Guillermo can't reply. He's doubled over the feeding trough, his eyes glassy, and he's started to vomit bile.

6

The stream that runs through the woods at Las Loberas has its source in the snowfields on the upper slopes of Peña Barga. It tumbles down the vertical waterfall on Mount Morana – crashing on to the blades of the hydroelectric turbines – then flows to the north of Peña Illarga, through carpets of thick moss and wild chestnut trees, seeking out the watermill at Pontedo, finally meeting the nearby River Susarón.

The stream that runs through the woods at Las Loberas has created dizzying gullies and torrential waterfalls, rapids, wild gorges and pools of black foam along its course. Occasionally you will also find calm stretches of still water where the trout gather on summer nights under the full moon.

Gildo, up to his waist in the water, appears out of the reeds. 'Here, Ángel, pass me the basket.' He's holding a trout. He rips off its head with his teeth and throws it on to the grass on the riverbank. 'This river is full of trout,' he says. 'You keep watch.'

Gildo disappears back into the reeds. He goes underwater and takes up the search again. I stay on the riverbank, keeping watch over the basket and the night. Keeping watch over the moon that is trembling at my feet like a dead trout.

*

When we get back to the cave Ramiro is already there, waiting for us with the latest news he's heard on the radio.

He had gone down to listen to it with Julio, the road mender, in Ancebos. Julio's old radio had miraculously escaped numerous searches, and one rainy night, exactly eight weeks ago, we'd listened in awe to that same radio as we heard the announcement that the war was definitively over.

'The borders are still closed,' says Ramiro, 'and all the trains and roads are being watched. Our only option is to stick it out for a bit longer.'

Gildo and I listen to him without much interest. We both already knew what Ramiro was going to tell us. House-to-house searches and summary executions. Exactly the same as we have always heard ever since we took to the hills.

Gildo skewers six trout on a piece of wire and props them up by the fire to cook. He cleans and salts the rest of them and takes them outside the cave to let them dry in the mountain air. 'Our only option is to stick it out for a bit longer,' he says, looking at Ramiro with a smile on his face.

*

When we've finished eating, Gildo and Ramiro take off their boots and jackets, light up a cigarette each and stretch out on their mattresses close to the fire.

It's four in the morning, and tonight it's my turn to keep watch until dawn.

Sitting at the mouth of the cave with my balaclava pulled down over my face and the submachine-gun resting across my legs it isn't long before I hear them breathing deeply and their regular, monotonous heartbeats before they nod off to sleep. Gradually

65

the mountain starts to regain the perfection of its shadows and mysteries, the primitive order created in front of my eyes by the night and the fire. Gradually everything becomes buried under the profound weightlessness of silence. Even this cold moon, stuck like a knife in the middle of the sky, keeps dragging me back to what my father said to me by the cemetery one night as we were returning home.

'Look, Ángel, look at the moon. It's the sun of the dead.'

*

At dawn I hear the cry of an eagle taking flight, the violent blow of an axe and the loud crash of a tree being felled, its branches being slowly ripped away from its trunk.

And so on, one after another, until a pool of clear sky is formed in the middle of the beech grove.

*

At eight in the morning, under the clear blue morning sky the woodcutters stop for breakfast. Sitting on a tree trunk they watch us appear from between the beech trees, trying not to show how uncomfortable our weapons make them feel.

The foreman offers us a drink from his wineskin. 'It's not very good,' he apologizes. 'The boy left it out in the sun, and it got warm.'

The boy doesn't say a word. The boy, a lad of thirteen or fourteen, has been watching silently since we arrived with a mixture of fear and admiration.

The wine tastes of the mountain and damp leather. It has a rancid smell of stale herbs that have been stored away for too long. But it can still quench our thirst from the early-morning sun.

'We brought it from La Moraña down in the valley,' the foreman explains. 'We're from the Valselada sawmill. We've only been here a couple of days.'

The woodcutters' tent is close by. It's just a few blankets draped over some poles, which they can set up and take down again from day to day, depending on where their work takes them.

They say we are the first people they've seen since they arrived.

'Who do you mean?'

The foreman looks puzzled. 'You.'

Ramiro gives him a menacing smile. 'Us? We're not here. No one's seen anyone,' he says. 'No one at all. Do you understand?'

The foreman understands. He nods his head while his companions sit there in complete silence. A silence that stretches, pregnant with fear, until they see us finally disappear into the trees.

Then, still close by, we hear the boy asking, 'That was them, wasn't it? The men from the hills?'

He is half contented, half scared, as if a pack of wolves had just passed by without harming him.

*

At the top of Láncara Pass, near the Nogares spring, a flock of sheep grazes, looking like a clump of wool stretched out to dry in the sun. They arrived at Cereceda on the train yesterday, crossed the fields through La Llánava and Candamo and climbed the old drovers' path that goes up to the pass, up to the high summer pastures and sheepfolds.

The shepherd must have been expecting us ever since he arrived and spread out his blanket on the grass.

*

Near the stone cabin several lambs are licking balls of salt in a hollowed-out trunk supported on trestles at each end. The mastiffs are higher up, with the flock, but a sheepdog with a mottled brown coat and a bored expression comes out of the barn when she sees us appear at the end of the fence and starts to bark.

Immediately a man peers out of the cabin door. The dog goes and stands beside him, and both of them watch us as we approach.

'You keep a close eye on your patch,' says the shepherd, as we get to the cabin.

'That's why we're still alive,' replies Ramiro, looking inside the cabin through the half-open door.

'Don't worry,' the shepherd smiles. 'You're my first visitors.' The shepherd, as always, is happy to see us. He's not afraid of us. He was born and bred in the mountains, like we were, and he's helped us out on more than one occasion.

Every summer, as soon as he arrives, he gives us the best lamb from his flock.

'I've been fixing it up a bit,' he says, going back into the cabin. 'This winter part of the roof caved in with the snow.' There's a gaping hole in the dark straw thatch, and a column of smoke, rising from the blackened pan in which the shepherd is cooking his meal, spirals up towards the sky.

'Migas,' he says. 'I put the bread out to soak last night and left it to soften up under the stars. You've come at just the right time.'

The shepherd fishes out four spoons from an old box and we all sit down around the pan. The dog flops down beside her master, intoxicated by the pungent aroma that has spread throughout the room.

'To tell you the truth, I wasn't sure you'd be here,' says the shepherd.

'Have you such little faith in us?'

'Just a tiny bit. But this year, now the war's over, even less. I thought that if you hadn't escaped the three of you would be pushing up daisies by now in some ravine.'

Gildo smiles as he sinks his spoon into the pan. 'You'll have to blame the wolf for a few more lambs before that happens,' he says.

'Believe me, nothing would give me greater pleasure.'

As we eat the sun, now level with top of the pass, begins to slip through the hole in the roof made by the snow. After a whole night on watch and with sleep clutching at my eyes like ivy, its warm yellow embrace feels comforting on my skin, which carries a pungent aroma of thyme in its pores, mixing smoothly with the hot steam from the pan. Yes, it's a huge stroke of luck to be here, leaning against the cool stone slabs of the cabin, savouring the shepherd's cooking, listening to the crackling of the burning logs and a tired, friendly conversation that gradually fades away, the sound of bells as the sheep comb the mountain seeking out the fresh grass and broom flowers.

*

I don't know how long I've been asleep – six or seven hours, maybe more – but when I open my eyes the sun crashes against them like an avalanche of bruised, bitter grains of wheat.

I am alone in the shepherd's cabin. I listen out. Nothing. Just the sound of the sheep's bells a long way off. My body jars as I get up, like a battered tree trunk. From the doorway I finally see Ramiro and Gildo together with the shepherd, separating a lamb from the others at the saltlick. I hardly recognize them. They've both shaved off their beards, like they do every summer, using the sheep shears. The sun is blazing and hurts my eyes, but I can see the flock coming down the hillside, and they will soon reach the gate in the fence. It will soon be night. Again.

'Come on, Ángel,' Ramiro calls out to me. 'Let's go.'

At the door of the cabin there's a pail full of water. I dip my head in it. It feels like a sharp tongue, running through me like the thrust of a dagger.

*

When we get to Pontedo we split up. Ramiro stays behind, waiting for us on the hillside with the lamb, while Gildo and I go down to the village to carry out the raid we've been planning since yesterday. We need to build up supplies for the winter.

*

I run across to the fountain basin in the middle of the village square keeping my head down. It is filled with stars. I beckon to Gildo, and he runs over and flattens himself beside me under the jet of water falling implacably against the blue pool that contains the night itself, reflecting a sky that has been transformed suddenly into a huge drinking trough for dead animals.

There is light on the other side of the square. A weak light bulb silhouettes the frame of a window in front of us. It's Zurdo's canteen, which serves as the village shop in Pontedo. Gildo and I remember it well, with the wild vine around its porch, where the village girls would sit in their pinafore dresses on Sunday afternoons. The shop counter covered in a worn grey oilskin; the old wooden shelves brimming with bottles and jars of preserves and packets of beans; the light bulb hanging like a surreal fruit from a beam in the ceiling.

Zurdo's canteen, the village shop. Gildo and I burst in at the same time. As if we've arrived from the depths of the night and oblivion. As if thrown in by an avalanche of stars crashing through the door that I've just kicked open.

The four men who were happily chatting around a table turn towards us with shock and disbelief etched on their faces. Maybe they're trying to picture us still hiding in our cave on the hillside or buried under the hay in some anonymous hayloft. But, instinctively, they get up from their chairs and back away towards the window with their hands in the air. They stay there, motionless and very close together, watching silently as Gildo jumps over the counter and starts to fill a rucksack with tins and packets while I aim my submachine-gun at them from the doorway.

I know all four of them well: Zurdo, the canteen owner, fat and bloodstained under his black overalls; Emilio, the river watchman; Don Pedro, the town clerk, drunk already, like every night; Flavio, the blacksmith from –

'You bastards!' The cry explodes like a flash of lightning through the silence of the canteen. But, long before he manages to get the gun out from his jacket pocket, I have already guessed his plan from his eyes. Don Pedro, the alcoholic town clerk, his face contorted by wine and fury, had been twitching nervously behind his paunch, waiting for me to drop my guard. But the spray of bullets cuts across his throat from his chest to his chin and carries on up into the ceiling beams with a dull buzzing like a feverish swarm of bees. The town clerk drops to the floor like an overripe fruit, never once taking his eyes off me, his hand still buried in the inside pocket of his jacket, as if searching for his tobacco to roll the last cigarette of his life.

When Gildo and I rush out of the canteen, a shower of stars crashes through the open door and sinks into the dead man's eyes, still frozen open in shock.

*

'What happened? What happened back there?' Ramiro has come out to meet us on the hillside. He has heard the shots.

Gildo and I stop. We are short of breath, exhausted.

'I killed Don Pedro,' I say. 'The town clerk.'

Along the road to Cereceda a truck's yellow headlights are already piercing the entrails of the night, rushing towards us at high speed.

'Here come the *guardias*,' shouts Gildo. 'Come on, let's go!'

'Calm down, Gildo,' says Ramiro. 'They won't come up here now. They wouldn't dare.'

The truck reaches the streets of Pontedo and pulls up sharply outside the canteen. In the glare of the headlights, from the hillside we see the *guardias* jumping down from the truck and the two men who appear at the door, carrying the town clerk's mutilated body. They throw it in the back of the truck, which doesn't waste any time in turning around and heading back along the road to Cereceda.

The rest of the *guardias* go into the canteen.

'What have we done? My God! What have we done?' says Gildo.

Ramiro looks at him, coldly. 'Will you shut up?' he shouts. 'We've killed him, OK? We've killed him. He's dead. So leave the mourning to his widow.'

I'm standing in the middle of the heather, frozen. I'm listening to my own intermittent breathing, to the faraway barking of the village dogs and to the machine-gun burst that scythes back and forth endlessly across the throat of the town clerk.

'He was asking for it,' says Ramiro. 'If I'd been in your shoes I'd have done the same thing.'

'But you know what this means, Ramiro. Now there's no turning back.'

'There's never been any turning back,' Ramiro replies, looking at Gildo. 'You know that.'

7

The bell sounds at eight on the dot. The train, a steam engine and four old wagons, bunches up with a hoarse bellow, belches out a column of smoke and starts crawling down the track, taking with it the last shreds of the afternoon.

The station master waits on the platform until the train disappears from view. Then he looks at the clock on the wall, checks that there's no one still waiting on the platform and returns to his office with a satisfied look.

Another day over.

*

'Lina said that you wanted to see us.'

'Yes, but not here. It's not safe.' The station master used to work with Gildo's father and is beginning to show his age. He is pacing up and down the office nervously. Although the station is some distance away from the nearest houses in Candamo and is separated from the village by a green row of elm trees, he has locked the door, closed the shutter on the ticket window and turned out the light, leaving us in total darkness.

He insists that he wants to help us, provided he doesn't have to take any risks. 'I told your wife that I would fix the time and place for the meeting.'

What the station master doesn't know is that the reason we are here, now, is precisely to avoid a meeting set up in advance with the possibility of some unpleasant surprise. The fact that he's an old friend of Gildo's father is not enough of a guarantee for us.

'We'll be gone very soon,' says Gildo. 'Don't be afraid.'

With a resigned air, the station master picks up the coffee pot, which has been bubbling away on the stove. In the darkness, which my eyes are gradually getting used to, I watch him pour the contents into an aluminium cup and polish it off in one slug.

'OK then. Let's get it over with as soon as possible,' he says. 'There's an empty goods train leaving for Bilbao in a fortnight's time. The driver is completely trustworthy, and there'll be no military escort. If you agree, I will arrange to get you some railway uniforms and passes.'

Gildo glances at Ramiro and me questioningly. 'And after that?' he asks.

'I know someone who can take you across to France by boat. It won't be the first time he's done that sort of thing.'

Ramiro, who, like me, has not said a word, goes over to the ticket window and looks at the empty platform through the crack. Without turning around, he asks, 'How much?'

The station master hesitates, still holding the coffee pot. 'Remember that it has to be shared between the three of us: the engine driver, the man with the boat and me.'

'How much?' Ramiro asks again, his voice dry.

There's another brief moment of silence. The station master, instead of replying, goes to his desk and takes a blue envelope from the drawer. He takes out three flyers, which have been carefully folded, unfolds one of them and places it on the desktop.

Resident of La Llánava, in the Cereceda District, in the Province of León. Born on 8 August 1912. Single. Tall, athletic build, fair complexion, blue eyes and blond hair. School teacher, member of the illegal trade union (CNT) and enemy of the Glorious National Uprising. Member of the gang led by Ramiro Luna Robles, a.k.a. the 'One-Armed Bandit'. Guilty of the murder of Don Pedro Ituero Ituero, Town Clerk of Pontedo, as well as numerous acts of theft, robbery and banditry in the La Moraña District.

'The other two are yours,' says the station master, looking at Ramiro and Gildo. 'They're more or less the same. One of the *guardias* brought them here this afternoon and told me to put them up on the station noticeboard.'

Ramiro and Gildo don't even bother to read theirs. They look at me without saying a word, waiting for me to respond, but all I can do is stare at that piece of blue paper that carries my name and personal details in large letters and, at the bottom, the reward on my head. Fifty thousand pesetas.

'That's what we're asking. Fifty thousand each. Freedom instead of death, for the same price. I think that's fair.'

Ramiro stands there, staring at him. He hasn't stopped staring at him since we came in, watching for the slightest trace of treachery he might be hiding from us behind his words. Ramiro, still staring at him, asks him point blank, 'How do we know we can trust you?'

Just at that moment, we hear footsteps on the platform.

Instinctively, the four of us freeze, holding our breath. Ramiro has pointed his gun at the station master who, terrified, tries to convince us with his eyes that he has not betrayed us.

Outside, right by the door, we hear a voice.

'There's no light on. He must have left.'

But then there's a rap on the window.

Ramiro makes a sign to the station master to keep quiet. The four of us can hear the sound of our own hearts beating.

Then we hear the same voice again from the platform. 'There's no one here.'

And the other voice replies, 'Let's go.'

*

We wait at least five minutes without moving a muscle, in complete silence, listening to the footsteps move away, first along the platform and then along the track, heading towards Ferreras. In the darkness of the office Ramiro still has his handgun trained on the station master, whose face is now so pale it looks like a death-mask. He must have been on the verge of screaming in panic.

Ramiro is the first one to move. Slowly and without a sound he creeps over to the window, making a thorough inspection of the area around the station.

'They're by the level crossing,' he says at last. '*Guardias.*' Then, turning towards the station master, he says with a smile, 'Sit down. Don't be scared. Now we know we can trust you.'

*

Gildo's house is on the edge of the village. It's higher up than the other houses in Candamo, perched on the hillside, beside the road to the cemetery. Gildo's house is the only one from which you can see the rooftops and lights of La Llánava in the distance. Perhaps that's why, when Gildo felt the time had come to get married, he brought Lina there.

Now that Gildo's parents are dead and he's had to escape to the hills, she lives there alone with their son, in the old house with its dark balcony and tiled chimney rising up like a lighthouse lost in the July night. Like so many other nights, Gildo must resign himself to watching her from a distance, reminding himself of the solitude in which his wife and son now live, while we make our way back past the cemetery, brimming with mint and moonlight, where his parents now sleep also in solitude.

*

'What do you think, Ramiro?'

Ramiro is smoking his cigarette in silence, stretched out on his mattress in the darkness. Gildo is outside on the rock, keeping watch. No one can get to sleep tonight.

'What about you?' he says, turning the question around.

'I don't know. This might be our last chance,' I say. 'I think we should take it.'

I wait for his reply but in vain. Ramiro stubs out his cigarette on the floor and turns his back to reflect on his uncertainty in private.

*

I open my eyes, and they are flooded with a huge puddle of blood. It's the sun glinting off Gildo's knife like a slaughtered beast.

I get up from the mattress and go to sit beside him. Gildo is whittling down a sprig of heather with his knife. Another one to add to the thousands of others he has whittled in the long, dead hours, all of them, without fail, ending up on the fire.

'Where's Ramiro?'

'Outside, having a wash,' says Gildo. 'He's just woken up.'

I roll a cigarette and smoke it in silence, contemplating the swathe of broom blazing in the July sun. The sky is perfectly clear, not a cloud in sight. The light is hard and blue. And there's a skylark singing in the middle of the broom. A skylark which never abandons us.

'I think we should wait,' says Gildo after a while.

'Wait? What for?'

'We've stuck it out here for two years. The worst years. This won't last for ever.' Gildo doesn't look at me as he speaks, as if he is totally engrossed in his work. But I detect a bitter note in his voice, a mixture of pleading and reproach. As if the situation we're in is all my fault.

'Look, Gildo. We're a lost cause. We lost the war. You know that as well as I do.'

'What I do know is that Franco is going to fall from power,' he says, looking at me finally. 'He can't last much longer.'

'I can't last much longer. I'm worn out, Gildo, you know? Worn out, beaten, desperate. I'm going to take this opportunity.'

Gildo pauses for a moment in silence, looking at me. Then he angrily throws the sprig he's been whittling into the patch of broom. 'It's easy for you two to go away,' he says, 'but I've got a wife and son down there all on their own.'

*

We eat our lunch in silence with no appetite.

The chance we have been waiting for, that we've dreamed about for so long, for so many days and years, has finally arrived. And now, strangely, we don't know what to do. It's not that we're scared of a strange country or a future we know nothing about. We're not even scared of being betrayed by the people helping us escape. It's our attachment to this lifeless land – lifeless and hopeless – which weighs down on us like a tombstone.

But we have to make a decision. I've been in favour all along. Gildo still has his doubts. What we don't know is what Ramiro thinks.

'OK,' he says finally, as if he has read my thoughts. 'Tonight we'll send word to Lina so they can start getting everything ready.'

Gildo looks at us, disappointed. He's on his own, and he knows it. He also knows that he can't survive here on his own.

But he still clings to one last hope. 'You still haven't said where you're going to find a hundred and fifty thousand pesetas.'

'I know,' says Ramiro. 'I know where we can find the money.'

8

The car goes past the mine with its sheds and slagheaps on the outskirts of Ferreras, crosses the bridge over the river and turns off smoothly down the narrow lane that, lined on either side with ash trees, runs along the riverbank out towards the fields.

Finally, after some three hundred metres, the headlights light up a stone wall against the night sky and, behind it, a large old house standing proudly on its own. The car stops in front of the gate, and a uniformed chauffeur gets out to open it. Then he goes back and drives the car carefully into the grounds.

Don José, the mine owner, gets out from the back seat. He has a quick look at the fruit trees bathed in moonlight, picks up his briefcase and, with an air of satisfaction, walks towards the front door where his wife and two daughters have come out to greet him. It is the same ritual every night, the invariable routine of a man in full control of his own life and his own time as well as those of all his loved ones.

The chauffeur, meanwhile, puts the car in the garage, between the ivy hedges and the still pool.

But, when he goes back to the entrance to lock the gate, he comes face to face with Ramiro's silent gun.

*

The hall light is still on and the front door still open. It clicks shut behind us with a practised smoothness.

'Is that you, Poldo?

Gildo's submachine-gun stifles the maid's scream before it starts, while Ramiro and I run down the hallway looking for the owners of the house.

They are standing in the dining-room, on either side of the table, which stretches out under a large chandelier. The table is laden with white porcelain, and there is a scent of freshly poured wine. They are standing there as if they were expecting us for dinner.

But when they see us in the doorway the woman reaches for her two daughters and instinctively pulls them tight to her.

'Take them out of here.'

The girls come with me without a struggle. They are too small to understand what is happening. I leave them in the kitchen with Gildo, who is watching the chauffeur and the maid.

When I get back to the dining-room, Ramiro is giving instructions to the mine owner, his former boss. 'You've got two minutes to get ready.'

'Get ready? What for?'

'You're coming with us.'

He tries to keep control of himself. 'Where are you taking me?' he asks.

'Two minutes,' says Ramiro drily. 'You've already had one.'

The woman throws her arms around her husband. 'What are you going to do to him?' she shouts. 'Don't go, José! Don't go! They'll kill you!'

The mine owner just stands there, staring at Ramiro. As if he recognizes him. Then, suddenly, he reacts. He disentangles himself from his wife's embrace and goes towards the coat-stand to fetch his jacket.

Ramiro steps forward to search the pockets. 'Listen very carefully,' he says to the woman, turning towards the door. 'Listen very carefully and do exactly what I say if you want to see your husband alive again. You've got until Friday to get hold of two hundred thousand pesetas. In small notes. On Saturday, at six in the morning on the dot, get in the car and head towards Tejeda. Just you and the chauffeur. Do you understand? We will be waiting for you somewhere along the road.'

The woman nods mechanically without taking her eyes off her husband.

'Do what he says, Elena,' he says, kissing her coldly on the cheek. 'And don't be afraid. If anyone asks after me, tell them I'm away in Madrid. It will all work out fine, you'll see.'

The woman watches us leave in silence, impotent, collapsing in a faint on the table like a rag doll.

*

When I wake up the sun has already fallen behind the beech trees. It slides smoothly across the grass, lifting a curtain of green mist in front of my eyes.

Ramiro is sleeping near by, stretched out on a blanket. Beyond him, Gildo is leaning against a beech tree, keeping watch over the mine owner and the paths that lead up the hillside.

'What time is it?'

'Eight o'clock.' It's Don José who replies. He's sitting in between us with his hands tied behind his back, gazing into the distance.

'Ramiro will relieve you at twelve,' says Gildo, spreading out his blanket on the grass in order to get some sleep.

'Is there any food left?'

'There's some cheese and dried beef. Over there, in my knapsack. Give him some, too.'

The mine owner has dropped his usual indifference to the change of guards. He clearly seems to prefer my company to that of Gildo.

In the distance, over by the pass at Amarza, night is falling. The mountains are blurred on the horizon like clouds of smoke, and an explosion of blue birds scatters across the shadowy beech groves.

'Breathtaking, isn't it?' He has spoken without looking at me. He's keen to start a conversation, but he doesn't dare to do it openly. The mine owner cannot forget (even if my submachine-gun let him) the unbreachable gulf that separates us.

'I'm used to it,' I reply.

He is silent again, gazing at the horizon, worried that he's offended me.

I roll a cigarette for each of us. I untie his hands so that he can smoke and he nods in thanks. Whatever happens, with night falling and not knowing where we are, even if he could escape he wouldn't get very far, and he knows it.

So he lights up his cigarette and sits there, watching the smoke melt lugubriously into the forest mist.

'Ever since I was a boy', I say, 'I've felt attracted to the mountains. The fire, the wind, the rivers, they're all alive, always moving. But the mountains, they're always the same, always peaceful and silent. They're like dead animals.'

The mine owner looks at me in surprise. He was clearly not expecting an explanation like that from someone who, as far as he knows, is nothing more than a thug, hiding like a wild animal in the very mountains he's talking about.

'You're the schoolteacher from La Friera, aren't you?' I look at him without replying, and he drops his gaze to the floor, as if he had said something inappropriate. 'People say a lot of things about you,' he continues apologetically.

'Not very nice things, I imagine.'

'You know as well as I do. Some people think that you're just common thieves and murderers. And others, on the quiet, think of you as poor wretches who are just trying to stay alive.'

'What do *you* think?'

He didn't expect such a direct question. Don José shifts uncomfortably on the grass and finishes off his cigarette before he replies. 'Nobody should be killed.'

He looks at me for a moment, watching for my reaction.

'Does that include us?'

'Of course it does. I mean nobody.'

'Well, that's not what you've said previously in public.'

Even though it's getting increasingly dark in the beech grove I can make out the brightness trapped in his eyes and the sudden faint tremor of his lips. It's the first time he's lost control of himself since we've been on the mountain.

I tie his hands behind his back again and sit down behind him, leaning against a beech tree, waiting for midnight.

'Take any domesticated animal, the best-behaved dog,' I say to him after a while, 'lock it in a room and beat it. You'll see how he turns and bites you. You'll see that he'd kill you if he could.'

The mine owner doesn't reply. He can't reply. Motionless on the grass, he looks like just another tree trunk among all the trees in the beech grove.

*

Santiago lives in Quintana, a small village hidden among poplars at the foot of the Peña Malera. Santiago is one of Ramiro's former workmates and one of the most trustworthy contacts we've had since we've been hiding in the hills. He's forty years old, and all he has to show for it is a pair of oxen, a handful of goats and half a dozen children who are still barely old enough to help their mother tend to the animals and the vegetable plot.

So, every day, while the stars are still shining in the sky above Quintana, Santiago takes out his bicycle and, come rain or shine, or even come snow, he covers the fifteen kilometres that separate him from Ferreras to go down Don José's mine.

And he doesn't get home until nightfall.

Today, however, on his way back to Quintana, halfway along the road that climbs up from Vegavieja, Santiago has heard an owl scream in the oak grove.

He stops immediately. He looks around him into the shadows of the night for a few moments and then he turns his bicycle lamp off and on three times.

Finally he turns it off when he sees me appear at the side of the road.

'Santiago.'

'Hello, Ángel.'

'Why are you so late today?'

'I got delayed in the pharmacy in Vegavieja getting some things for Consuelo.'

Consuelo is his wife. A dark woman, who is unwell. A woman who, like all the women in this country, is old before her time.

'Did you see anything?'

'No, nothing unusual. At least, not at the mine.'

'What about at the barracks?'

'The same. I don't think Don José's wife has reported anything.'

Santiago constantly looks from side to side, watching the road. His tired eyes, sharpened by the mine, could spot anyone hiding in wait among the night's motionless shadows from a long way off.

'It's tomorrow, isn't it?' he asks.

'Six o'clock. You might pass the car on your way down.'

'I wish you the best of luck, Ángel.'

The bicycle lamp lights up the road again.

'Santiago.' He turns around to look at me. 'We may not see each other again. At least, not for a long time.' The words weigh on my heart like heavy stones, making it hard to say goodbye when, as we both know, this could be the last time. 'I want to thank you for everything.'

Santiago shakes my hand without speaking and goes off, pushing his bicycle along the road.

*

The mine owner looks at his watch again nervously and anxiously examines the black ribbon of road.

'It's time,' he says. 'They should have been here already.'

He shows me his gold pocket watch with its hands pointing to half past six.

'Do you trust your wife?'

'Completely.'

'Do you trust her not to have talked to anyone?'

He hesitates a moment before he replies, 'Of course.'

'Well then, relax.'

It's still night-time over the hills of Vegavieja. Clouds of stars hang over the river that runs at our feet with a deep moan. It's cold as well. Much too cold to bear on this long, tense wait.

'You know the drill,' says Ramiro, once again. 'Gildo, you wait in the road and stop the car. Ángel will keep you covered from the shelter. We've got to do this as quickly as possible.'

As he speaks, a car's headlights appear in the distance, on the horizon, ripping the fog from the river.

'Lie down.'

The mine owner rushes to obey. Ramiro takes out his handgun and squats down beside him in the heather.

'Good luck,' he says, as Gildo and I start to climb down to the road.

*

Gildo holds up his hand to stop the car.

The car brakes sharply and pulls over to the side of the road, just in front of the road-menders' shelter where I've taken cover.

'Turn off the lights.'

They do as they are told, and the dawn's milky darkness stretches over the road again.

Now a door opens, and Don José's wife gets out from the back seat with a bag in her hand. Inside the car, there is just the hazy silhouette of the chauffeur, sitting at the wheel.

Gildo starts to approach, all the time pointing his submachine-gun at the woman. 'Throw me the bag,' he orders. 'Throw it to me and go and stand at the side of the road.'

They are the last words he'll ever speak. Because, just at that moment, the woman throws herself to the floor and starts shooting at him. Almost simultaneously, the unexpected roar of several submachine-guns provides backup from inside the car.

I take too long to react. Firing through the open doorway from the back of the shelter, I can feel the screech of the bullets in my throat as they blindly seek out the car's silhouette, the woman's body on the road, the darkness of the dawn and death. As if the submachine-gun and not me was the first to get over the surprise.

Suddenly, I realize that no one is firing back. That I'm alone in the middle of the night firing endless bullets into several dead bodies.

'Gildo!'

The silence explodes in my ears like a final shot.

The car is tilted clumsily over a burst tyre. Near by, the bodies of Gildo and Don José's wife lie mutilated on the road.

'Gildo!'

I run to him without even bothering to search the car in case there was someone there who could still shoot at me.

Gildo is lying in a big puddle of blood, staring at the sky, his body riddled with bullets and his eyes full of stars.

'What happened, Ángel? What happened?' Ramiro runs down the slope, with his gun trained on the mine owner.

I don't need to explain. He stops in the middle of the road, motionless, stunned, with his eyes fixed on Gildo's body. His eyes are vacant.

'He didn't want to go,' he says in a very low voice, as if speaking to himself.

Suddenly, almost at the same time, we both have the same thought. Ramiro goes up to the woman's mutilated body and turns it over with his foot. A headscarf and a wig spill on to the road. Despite the black hole where his left eye used to be, we both easily recognize the unmistakeable face of the captain of the Ferreras barracks.

Terrified, the mine owner has started to back away towards the car, where the inert bodies of more *guardias* are slumped.

But Ramiro's shot goes straight through his heart and plasters him against the car door.

Part Three
1943

9

The door opens smoothly, and the silhouette of Ramiro's mother, silent and dressed in mourning, is framed in the doorway, lit up by the moon.

She stands there for a while, listening out for any sound, trying in vain to see anything in the thick darkness of the bakery.

'Mother, we're over here.'

She closes the door and makes her way tentatively towards us, guided only by memory and instinct, between the chests and sacks and the sinister outlines of the baskets hanging from the beams. 'Are you all right?'

'Yes, Mother, we're all right. How about you?'

'What kept you so long?'

'We couldn't come any earlier. The *guardias* were out in the lane.'

She looks at us from the depths of her eyes. They are bright with hope, as if once more making sure that the miracle is true and we are still alive. Making sure that we are not ghosts emerging every now and then from the shadows of the bakery to carry on feeding her hope. 'I was so worried.'

'Why?'

'I haven't heard anything about you for a month.'

In the silence of the bakery it seems as if the words exchanged between Ramiro and his mother are mangled by the night and the smoke before they reach my ears. It's as if they'd been spoken years before in some distant place from which the sun had disappeared for ever and not in this dark, forgotten room tacked on to the side of the stables at the end of the yard, which still retains the sacred memory of bread in its old flour chests and the indelible imprint of all the men who have lived in this house.

'Are you hungry?'

'No.'

'Your sister brought this tin of tobacco for you yesterday,' she says.

'How are they?'

'They're well. Worried, of course, like me.'

'Tell them we've been here.'

While we're speaking, Ramiro's mother puts the tin of tobacco in my rucksack, together with a loaf of bread and some pieces of dried meat. Then she rummages in the heap of dried heather next to the oven.

'Here're the boots,' she says, bringing over a small package. 'I've had them here since Sunday.'

Ramiro runs his hand over them. He almost caresses them. Then he sits down on a chest to puts them on.

'These are good boots,' he says. 'They'll last us at least a couple of winters.'

His mother kneels down in front of him to help him tie up his laces. She must be thinking exactly the same thing as us. These boots, hidden under the cover of the night, could be the last ones that La Llánava's old cobbler has to make for us. But she doesn't say anything. She just looks at us in silence with the distant, expressionless look of a woman who is used to lying awake every night, waiting, in the terrible solitude of a big empty house, for the furtive arrival of her son.

And then to watch him leave, always in a hurry, before she's even had time to look at him properly.

'Stay for a while. Have something to eat before you go.' Always the same words. The same helpless expression every time.

'Mother, you know I can't stay here a moment longer than I absolutely have to,' says Ramiro once again. 'The *guardias* could turn up any minute. More than anything, I don't want to put you in any danger.'

She looks at him, broken-hearted. 'When will you be back?'

'I don't know, Mother, I don't know. Whenever.'

Before we leave I throw my old boots through the oven door into the hot ashes. They were completely worn out, the soles flapping and rotten through.

They were the ones that Gildo had been wearing when he died.

*

'Why didn't you tell her?' Ramiro, lying beside me on the grass, looks at me, puzzled. 'Why didn't you tell your mother?' I ask him.

He hesitates for a moment before he replies. 'What for? It's better that she never finds out. That way she'll keep on hoping for ever.'

He falls silent again, listening to the night's heartbeat, calm, monotonous and profound.

We have been here for almost an hour, hidden in the orchard behind the priest's house. Don Manuel has gone to the bar, like he does every night, to listen to the radio or play cards.

*

Finally, towards midnight, we're tipped off by a dog barking at the end of the alleyway.

Ramiro and I flatten ourselves on the grass and listen with all our senses on alert. The breeze through the orchard has settled down, and on the other side of the wall we can hear footsteps coming up the street and voices exchanging the customary greetings, like any other night.

'See you in the morning.'

Don Manuel still doesn't know that for him this is not going to be like any other night. Don Manuel, the village priest in La Llánava, still doesn't know, as the door creaks open, that behind him, in the light of the moon shining on the roof of his house, lurks the dull throb of revenge.

*

He has brought us into his office without saying a word. The room is dominated by a crucifix, with a table at the end and a few books scattered on a bookshelf on the wall.

He invites us to sit down with a nod.

'No, you sit down,' Ramiro tells him.

Don Manuel crosses the room and sits down in his chair behind the table. He gathers up the sleeves of his cassock and clasps his hands together, watching us all the time.

I look at his ageing face under the dim light of the bulb. His hair is completely grey, as if scorched, and his white hands are trembling, perhaps more than usual, out of fear. There is nothing left of his former robustness, that inexhaustible energy that he used to control the religious lives of everyone in La Llánava, and perhaps their private lives, too. Nor, of course, of his unusual and feverish enthusiasm for denouncing suspects in the village when the war came knocking at everyone's door.

A long time has passed since then. A long time for everyone.

'Why are you trembling, Don Manuel?' asks Ramiro, with a hard, icy smile. 'You wouldn't be scared of us, would you?'

'Of course I am,' he replies, with a steady voice. Then, after a short silence, he looks at me. 'I'm just waiting for you to tell me to what it is that I owe the pleasure of your visit.'

'It's been a long time since we last met, Don Manuel,' I say. 'Not since before the war.'

I've put great emphasis on those last few words, but he doesn't seem to have noticed. Now that he's got over the initial shock, he leans back in his chair, trying to look relaxed, although the tense muscles straining in his face and neck still betray his anxiety.

'Do I need to spell out the fact that I don't enjoy your company?'

'No,' replies Ramiro. 'We thought as much.'

'So?'

'We've come here to kill you.'

Don Manuel's hands suddenly stop trembling, and his face is gripped by an intense, icy pallor.

My submachine-gun, pointing at his eyes, forces him to refrain from his initial impulse to stand up.

'But, before that, you're going to tell us everything you know.'

'Everything I know about what?'

'Everything,' Ramiro repeats. 'Everything you know.'

Don Manuel looks to me pleadingly. His eyes are bulging, shot through with panic.

Ramiro sits down in front of him.

'I'm going to help you out,' he says. 'You can start by telling us about my brother.'

'Your brother?' the priest splutters, his voice trembling.

'Yes, my brother. You remember him, right?'

'Of course, of course. How could I not remember him? Juan. He died in the war –'

'No, not in the war,' Ramiro interrupts brusquely. 'My brother died here, in La Llánava. You know that full well.'

'Do I?'

Ramiro stares at him without replying.

'I don't know anything about your brother or anyone else,' says the priest.

'Don't lie to us, Don Manuel. We're like God. We can see everything from up there on high.'

But Don Manuel does not reply. He stares fixedly at the table to avoid our eyes. He must be wondering how we have managed to discover something that has been kept secret for so many years.

'I'll refresh your memory for you,' says Ramiro, fiddling with his gun with apparent nonchalance, but his voice is overlaid with notes of barely controlled anger. 'Do you remember one night, about six years ago, when a man knocked at your door asking for help?'

'There have been so many times that people have come to my house asking for help,' says the priest, defending himself clumsily. 'Don't forget, I'm a priest.'

Under the black shadow of the crucifix his words sound strange and unreal, almost like an insult.

'You know perfectly well which night I'm talking about.'

'No, I don't.'

'Then I'll tell you.'

Don Manuel looks at Ramiro with his eyes out on stalks. A cold, sticky sweat runs down his face when Ramiro says to him,

'That man was wounded. That man was my brother, and he asked you to hide him here in your house.'

'I couldn't do that, Ramiro,' the priest replies, now completely boxed in. 'I couldn't hide him. I would have been compromised myself.'

'And you handed him over to his pursuers so that they could finish him off.'

The priest has stopped trying to defend himself; he's stopped saying anything. His hands, gripping the edge of the table, look like white vine shoots and his frozen lips are trembling like blood-stained leaves as he mutters a prayer.

'Stand up! Stand up and shut up. Praying won't do you any good!'

*

Out on the streets of La Llánava, only the dogs and the moon are awake. The dogs see us off, barking until we reach the outskirts of the village, but the moon doesn't abandon us, happy to stay with us all night long.

Don Manuel walks along without saying a word, looking down at the ground, his hands buried in his cassock like a strange ghost drifting away towards the river. Ramiro and I follow him at a short distance, one on each side of the path, with our guns trained on him constantly.

Once we reach the riverbank the priest turns on to the path that leads up through the poplar trees to the old plank bridge. A couple more turns around the last fields in the village, right on the riverbank, and we come out into the pastures at Remolina.

'Here?'

Don Manuel nods.

I look at the dark, waterlogged meadow, covered in watercress. The sombre shadows of the poplar trees stretch out over it. The river runs alongside it with a deep roar. The night is so perfectly balanced that there's nothing to suggest that Juan is buried here under the grass. Under this same grass over which Ramiro and I have traipsed so many times, so many nights, on our way down to La Llánava.

Don Manuel stands beside us, in silence.

'Kneel down,' says Ramiro.

In a gesture of desperation Don Manuel has torn off a branch from a hawthorn bush and stuck it in the ground, like a cross.

He refuses to obey the order. He's clearly afraid that once he's in that position, on his knees, defenceless, we'll carry out our threat and put a bullet in his head.

'Kneel down!' Ramiro shouts. 'Kneel down and pray, you piece of shit. There's a man buried under here, not a dog.'

The breeze gently rustles through the bulrushes and the branches of the poplar trees. For a moment it drowns out the roar of the river. In the middle of the field a cold, distant moon lights up the outline of the priest kneeling in front of the hawthorn branch and the gun that is pointing at the back of his head.

*

I am roused at dawn by barking in the distance and Ramiro's voice in the darkness.

'Did you hear that?'

The two of us lie there wordless, motionless, holding our breath.

The barking is some distance away, up in the pass. But it's still only daybreak, and at this time of the morning the flocks will still be waiting for the church bell to toll before leaving La Llánava.

'They're coming,' shouts Ramiro, jumping up from his bedding.

We can see them from the entrance to the cave. The *guardias* are coming up the side of the mountain, fanned out, already quite close to the pass. There are twenty or thirty of them, and they've brought along a few dogs. In the milky light of dawn their capes are floating, green and unmistakeable, over the thicket.

I crawl out of the cave, and, very slowly, trying not to make any sound, I bend the branches of the nearest broom bushes over the entrance. Ramiro keeps hold of them from inside the cave and ties them together with a piece of string.

'Can you see anything?'

'No. That's fine like that.'

I crawl back through the broom bushes, into the cave. The *guardias* are now up in the pass.

I tie the other end of the string to a nail in the wall, by the entrance. I let go and the broom sways gently for a few seconds before becoming completely still. Now nobody on the outside would ever be able to find the mouth of the cave or even guess that it's there.

'I should have killed him,' says Ramiro, as he sprinkles the broom with brandy to distract the dogs. 'I should have killed him and thrown him in the river.'

I pick up my submachine-gun, and Gildo's as well, and lie face down beside him.

*

They've spent the whole morning combing the entire hillside. They went right up to the peak and set fire to the heather on the La Roza hill in case we were hiding there.

They've passed right by us several times.

At midday, bored and tired, the *guardias* regroup on the pass and start to make their way back down to La Llánava.

The shutters are closed on all the windows in the village and not even the dogs are out on the streets. Two dark trucks are parked in the square, waiting for the *guardias*, and inside their houses, huddled in their kitchens, the villagers will be waiting for the violent knock on the door any time now, ordering them to open up.

It's been like this for six years now, living in silence, terrified, torn between pity, which moves them to help us, and the ever-increasing fear of reprisals.

10

The man is coming up towards us in the middle of the road, whistling a tune and pulling at the reins without much enthusiasm. He is wearing an old sheepskin coat, stained by the years and the rain, and a felt hat pulled down to his eyes.

Maybe that's why he doesn't see us until he's practically on top of us.

It's not yet eight o'clock on a day that started out with the sky swollen with black clouds, threatening rain. Up here, on the mountain pass at Amarza, the dampness and light are fused together, forming a single substance, a cold and sticky fog that gently saturates the ground and the atmosphere alike.

When he sees us, standing in the middle of the road just after a bend, the man pulls on the reins and draws to a halt. As Ramiro and I approach he looks suspiciously at the nearby beech groves from beneath the brim of his hat to see if there are any more of us.

He accepts my greeting with a look of mistrust, but his eyes, buried beneath his hat, do not betray the slightest shadow of fear.

'We have been waiting for you,' I say.

The man doesn't reply. All he does is look at us, motionless beside his horse. He knows who we are (Ramiro's mangled arm is a giveaway) but, recently, there have been groups of *guardias* and mercenaries combing the hills dressed like us and carrying the same type of weapons, hoping either to take us by surprise or, at least, spread confusion and fear among our network of contacts, and he clearly wants to make sure of his ground.

I go up to the horse and turn back the blanket covering the two bags strapped to the saddle. 'What are you carrying?'

'Flour', he replies, tersely.

'Where from?'

'Vegavieja.'

I untie one of the bags and plunge my hand inside. When I pull it out it's completely white, covered in flour.

Ramiro nods his head. We also wanted to make sure.

'The Frenchman wants to see us,' I say, finally.

It's the password he's been waiting for. The man slowly lifts the brim of his hat to look us up and down again. Then he looks up at the rainclouds, which are now hovering twice as big over the green tops of the beech trees, and leads his horse off the road.

*

We've been marching in silence the whole way, following the man at a distance. Although we're going in the opposite direction, this is the same road we came along years back with Gildo and Ramiro's brother, fleeing from a war that was lying in wait for us on the other side, too. As we pass by the crumbling walls of the sheepfold where, all that time ago, we came across an abandoned dog, I think back to that night, and I can remember it so clearly, it feels so recent, that every other night, including last night, seem to me to be one and the same endless night of fog and lynched dogs.

Around ten o'clock we glimpse a farmhouse lost among the

beech groves. It is the first sign of life we have seen since we came over the top of the pass and crossed into Asturias.

'You stay here,' says the man, waiting for us to catch up. 'I'll go down first and make sure everything's OK. If I appear at the window it means you can come down.'

It's been a while since the clouds burst, and now a gentle, melancholy drizzle is falling softly against the beech trees and the wild blueberry bushes scattered across the couch grass. Ephemeral droplets of cold water tremble on the berries.

Sheltering from the rain under a beech tree, Ramiro and I watch the man cross the meadow, tie up his horse in the open-sided barn and go into the house.

Luckily it is not long before he appears at the window.

*

Ramiro and I have been hidden in the stable all day, lying on a heap of straw, with only the horse for company.

The owner of the farmhouse and his wife (who we managed to glimpse, just for a moment, through the window) come and go, seeing to the household chores. Occasionally, as they pass by the barn, they throw a furtive glance towards the stable.

According to our informants (Marcial, the miller from Vegavieja, acted as our go-between) the couple have no children and live up here on their own, earning what they can from the smallholding and the husband taking goods and travellers across from one side of the pass to the other. Because he knows these mountains like the back of his hand and because he spent two years in prison after the war building up a bitter hatred, he is the most loyal and the bravest go-between for the fugitives in the area.

*

'There are fewer and fewer of you holding out around here. Five or six men scattered across the Amarza Hills and two groups around Beres over towards Cabañada: the Acevedos and the Cariñosos. I suppose you've heard of them.' The man is sitting opposite us, eating his supper in the semi-darkness of the kitchen, illuminated only by the distant glow of the hearth. It's the only light in the farmhouse, which is lost in the mountains and is now being battered by the rain under a dark, starless night.

'Acevedo has crossed the pass a couple of times to carry out missions on the other side,' I tell him. 'As far as we know, he was the one who blew up the power line in Valselada. But, of course, the people down there blame us for it.'

The man looks indifferent and carries on talking. 'The *guardias* have been picking off the others one by one, either that or they've handed themselves in.'

'What about him? Who's he with?'

'Who do you mean? The Frenchman?'

'Yes.'

'He's on his own. In hiding. But he wants to link up all the groups in the area. He spent a couple of years with the Cariñosos before he went across to France. And now he's come back bringing weapons and orders.'

Ramiro, who has been silent all this time, listening, pushes his plate to one side and leans back on the bench. 'What sort of orders?' he asks.

'To go on the attack. For everyone to team up and attack at the same time. In France they think that Franco's days are numbered. They say that Hitler's about to fall, and once they've finished him off the Allies will also invade Portugal and Spain.'

Ramiro smiles at him sceptically. 'We've been hearing that

same song for years now. It the same old song that the politicians have been constantly singing over there, so that the handful of wretches who couldn't escape in time keep on sticking it out over here. And now, on top of that, they want us to attack!' Ramiro's voice gets louder and angrier as he speaks. 'You know, I only want one thing from the politicians. Guns. If they want to go on the attack, let them come over here. Let the politicians come up here to the mountains.'

The owner of the farmhouse shrugs his shoulders. 'My job is just to put you in touch,' he replies. 'After that, it's up to you and the Frenchman to sort things out between you.'

His wife, sitting beside him, doesn't say a word. She's not involved in our conversation. She's still young, much younger than her husband, but her face has the expression of an old woman with traces of melancholy or exhaustion. And she is embarrassed when she briefly looks across the table and suddenly, as if by accident, her eyes meet mine.

*

When we've finished our supper, the man puts on his sheepskin coat, picks up a torch and an umbrella and heads towards the stable to get his horse. Watching from the half-open window, I see him mount the horse and disappear into the night, heading up the mountain, under the rain.

'I'll be back in two hours,' he says as he leaves.

*

Ramiro, as always, doesn't trust anyone, and after finishing off his cigarette he takes a blanket and goes off to keep watch from the barn. So now it's just me and the woman, alone in the kitchen.

She clears up the plates and wipes down the table in silence, without looking at me, as if I had left, too. Then she brings a large pitcher of milk from the pantry and sits down next to the hearth and starts whisking it as she waits for her husband to return. It's something she's clearly done many times before in her life, and so, too, she must have spent many nights completely alone in this remote farmhouse.

In the magical backlight from the hearth, sheltered in the darkness that keeps me hidden from her sight, I can watch her deep-blue, melancholic eyes, her tortured lips, and I can also imagine, under the black shadow of her dress, her trembling breasts, so close to me and so defenceless, like her, and the warm caress of her legs around both sides of the pitcher as she whisks the milk with slow circular movements, her whole body moving in unison.

She must have read my thoughts, but she doesn't say anything. She carries on with her work as if completely oblivious to my presence, but, instinctively, she gathers the folds of her skirt between her knees.

Only after a long while, as the fire starts burning down to the ashes and the milk starts to curdle in the pitcher, she raises her eyes to look at me. 'It's been a long time since you've been with a woman, hasn't it?' She says it in a neutral, expressionless tone, her eyes searching me out in the shadows of the kitchen. Her words, the first she has spoken all day, hang in the air, floating between us, as if they had always been there.

I had dozed off. Drowsy from the meal and the heat of the fire, I had dozed off, and although her sudden attention has startled me I don't reply, and I stay there, slumped on the bench, not knowing how to respond and not finding sufficient courage to return her gaze.

She puts the pitcher of milk to one side.

'Come with me,' she says, getting up and going towards the door.

*

When I go into the room she's already sitting on the edge of the bed, waiting for me.

She welcomes me with a gentle moan. On our first contact she curls up into herself, as if she'd been run through with a knife. Slowly, without speaking to each other, I unbutton her dress. She lets me do it, sitting with her hands splayed out on either side of her half-open legs, her eyes fixed on mine. Kneeling, I kiss her shoulders and breasts furiously, my lips ablaze. My hands, moving clumsily across the mysterious territory hidden beneath her skirt, seek out the fire and passion of her thighs.

She can't resist any longer. Suddenly she doubles over on to herself, like a broken branch, and drags me to the floor, filling my eyes with black light. It's total night. Infinite vertigo. The vault of time begins to fall over us with the deafening roar of two rivers meeting. Two rivers meeting and fusing. The roar of two rivers meeting and fusing, meeting and fusing.

She stays beside me for a moment, naked, trembling. Then she gets dressed silently and goes out of the room, leaving me on my own.

When I return to the kitchen she is sitting back by the fire, her hair combed and tied back, whisking the milk in the pitcher again.

She doesn't even raise her eyes to look at me as I come in.

*

Around midnight I'm woken by the sound of a horse's hooves. They approach the farmhouse at a medium trot, splashing through the puddles.

Ramiro is still in the barn. The woman gives me a fleeting, expressionless glance, still sitting next to the fire. Maybe she fell asleep, too, waiting for her husband.

Without moving from the bench I pick up the submachine-gun and aim it towards the door.

*

Shortly afterwards the door opens abruptly.

However, it's not the husband who appears. It's Ramiro, holding his gun nervously.

'It came back on its own,' he says. 'The horse came back on its own.'

The woman and I have both stood up. She stands still beside the hearth for a moment, stunned, unable to believe what Ramiro has just told us. Then, suddenly, she charges towards the door, screaming.

'They've killed him. My God, they've killed him.'

Ramiro gives her a shove, pushing her back towards the back of the kitchen. 'Are you mad?' She looks at him, distraught, unable to comprehend. 'If they've killed him', says Ramiro, 'they'll already have surrounded the house. If you go outside you're going to get your head blown off.'

Through the crack in the shutter we can just about make out the spray of black rain drenching the barn.

'Where does that door lead to?' Ramiro asks the woman, pointing to the door behind us at the back of the kitchen.

'To the stable. We use it in the winter when it's snowing.'

'Is it unlocked?'

She looks for the key in the cupboard.

'Listen carefully,' Ramiro says. 'Get undressed and get into bed. Don't be scared. They won't do anything to you. We're going to try to get away from the house.'

The woman stays behind, alone in the kitchen, not knowing what to do, not knowing whether to scream or collapse, not knowing whether to hide in the darkest corner of the house or whether to run out in search of her husband.

The woman stays behind, alone in the kitchen, like a statue seized by panic.

*

There is complete darkness inside the stable. The cows are sleeping peacefully, and their heavy breathing fills the darkness with their hot breath. But we can't see them. We can just make out their silhouettes, lying down, in the muggy light from the window.

'They're out there,' says Ramiro, in a very low voice.

'How do you know?'

'I don't know how, but I can smell them.'

Outside, the silence has ripened like a fruit. Even the rain seems to have been silenced, waiting for the tragedy to unfurl. Sensing death.

'What do you think has happened?'

'I don't know,' says Ramiro. 'They must have caught them as they were coming back down. Someone must have spoken out of turn and they knew we were meeting here tonight.'

'What about the horse? Why would they let it go?'

'It must have escaped.'

Ramiro has suddenly gone quiet. In the darkness, only his heavy breathing betrays his presence.

'The horse,' he says. 'It's there, in the barn.' We can see its silhouette through the window and hear its rapid breathing after its gallop across the mountain. 'Cover me, Ángel. I'm going to try to grab it. It can help us get away from here.'

But the creaking of the door scares the horse, and before Ramiro can get close it canters out of the barn and goes off across the field at a trot.

Finally it stops, out of our reach, in the middle of the night and the rain.

'What shall we do, Ramiro? Why don't we leave?'

'We can't. If they are out there it would be suicide. We've only got one option.'

'What's that?'

'We have to wait.'

*

We don't have to wait very long.

Not long after making its escape the horse starts to come back to the barn. Behind it, prodding it forward, we can just make out two shadows in the darkness. Ramiro was right. We are surrounded.

'The whole area must be crawling with *guardias*.'

I don't know whether he is looking for an answer. I don't have one, in any case. I know as well as he does that there's no way out.

'What if we hide?'

'Where?'

We hear a voice, very close, behind the barn.

'They're already here.'

Ramiro crouches beside me, next to the window. 'Untie the cows,' he says.

'The cows?'

'Yes, hurry up. We're going to make them stampede.'

Gingerly, guided in the dark by the heavy breathing of the sleeping cows, I slip across to the row of stalls and start to undo their collars. The cows stand up lazily, heavily, surprised, creating a deafening throng of hooves in the middle of the stable.

I make my way back to Ramiro. 'How many are there?'

'I think there're six.'

'That should be enough.' Ramiro squints through the window. He's put his gun back in its holster and he's holding two hand-grenades. 'I'll throw one on either side. We've got to make the most of the confusion when they run out.'

I search for the cows in the darkness and start hitting them with my gun and kicking them on the legs and stomach so that they run out of the stable as soon as the door is open. The cows churn around, in shock.

Outside, the *guardias* will be wondering what on earth is happening inside the stable. They'll soon find out.

'Ready?' It's Ramiro, standing by the door.

'Ready,' I reply, holding my breath and crouching down between the cows.

I don't have time to say anything else. The door opens wide and the stampede drags me out of the stable. Almost at the same time a violent glare fills the barn. The horse rears up in front of me, up on its back legs, whinnying. It flattens me against one of the cows. The ground is cold and wet. A hoof stamps down on me, in the middle of my back. But then I'm back on my feet, I don't know how, and I'm running. I run through the night, through the bursts of submachine-gun fire. A cow falls flat on the ground. I turn around, opening fire into the night. Into the void, which is now ripped by another violent glare. Ramiro. Where is he? The submachine-guns have gone quiet. We have to run. Run desperately into the open night between the remaining cows. Between the rain and the screech of the bullets. Into the salvation of the beech trees, which can't be far away now. Which can't be far away and which, at last, close their dark fronds behind my back.

*

The morning light takes me by surprise, lying face down among some brambles, in the middle of the beech grove, with my heart pressed against the ground so that no one can hear its frenetic red beating. I don't even know how long I've been here or how far I am from the farmhouse and the boots of the *guardias*.

Nor, of course, do I know what's happened to Ramiro, and that's why I'm trapped here like a blinded animal in the middle of these brambles.

*

It must be nearly midday. I can tell, because it's stopped raining and a weak sun, far away and damp, is filtering through the beech trees, shedding a green light straight down on to my back.

I can't bear it here any longer. I've been lying in these brambles for eight or nine hours with my face flat against the ground, and I can hardly move at all. I can't bear it any longer. I'm getting out. I haven't heard one suspicious sound in the beech grove all morning, and, anyway, even if the *guardias* did follow my trail across the hillside they'll have given up by now. Or maybe not.

Or maybe they caught Ramiro, and they've gone off satisfied, leaving me for another time. I don't know. I only know that I have to get out of here, get out of these brambles and find somewhere safe from which I can see the farmhouse and find out what's happened.

Slowly, holding my breath and tensing all my muscles so as not to make the slightest sound, I begin to crawl through the brambles. The fresh grass is cold and wet. The hawthorns claw at my clothing angrily, scratching my arms and face. But I can now clearly see the surrounding terrain, the beech trees marching down the mountainside like a ghostly army of shadows. Dark, green, mysterious shadows, which may be hiding other shadows that are less passive, more twitchy, lying in wait for me. For a long while I scrutinize them one by one, looking for any movement, any glint of light, the slightest interruption in the stream of raindrops running down off the branches of the trees. Everything seems to be still. Slowly, very slowly, with my submachine-gun ready to obey my command, I crawl forward on my knees and elbows until I finally get free of the brambles. Stock-still and silent, I inspect the shadows again briefly and then crawl over to the nearest tree trunk and flatten myself against it as if I were a clump of moss.

The light is more intense, greener and more vertical here.

*

The first thing they did was bury the three cows in an enormous open trench in front of the barn. One of them was still alive, moaning and writhing on the grass until one of the *guardias* finished it off with a bullet.

They led away the other three, and the woman, tied to the

horse's tail. Draped over the horse itself were the bodies of two men, ripped apart by gunshots.

The blanket covering them meant that I couldn't make out whether one of them was Ramiro.

*

Now, night is falling across the mountains again. The shadows slide past, deep and thick. They fuse together, weaving themselves into an organic mass of rain and ferns, which slowly starts to take hold of the beech grove.

Soon the owl will begin hooting.

*

For several long hours, feverishly and sporadically, the owl has been hooting throughout all the beech groves, along all the paths and across all the pastures of the night. It's been hooting half-heartedly, tirelessly but half-heartedly, driven only by anxiety and despair.

And so, too, for several long hours, throughout all the beech groves, along all the paths and across all the pastures of the night, the only response has been a tenacious, tight-knit silence.

It was only at dawn, near the derelict sheepfold by the Amarza Pass, that the other invisible owl finally returned its call.

Almost immediately Ramiro appears between the walls. 'I knew you'd come through here sooner or later.'

Day has started to break and a sweet, milky light reveals a smile on his face.

'I wasn't so sure that I'd find you. I could see two bodies on the horse's back.'

'The owner of the farmhouse and the Frenchman. I guess it

must have been the Frenchman. They passed by very close.' Then, still smiling, he says, 'You know, you sound just like a real owl!'

'Yes, of course,' I say, leaning back against the wall, exhausted. 'And I can run just like a mountain goat, and I can hear just like a hare, and I attack with the cunning of a wolf. I'm the most skilful animal in all these hills.'

Ramiro feels inside his jacket for his tobacco tin. 'Roll me a cigarette,' he says. 'I haven't had a smoke all day.'

11

Autumn is here already, the end of a slow deep-crimson September which has given back to the mountains the ancient, profound solitude that the summer briefly destroyed.

Autumn is here already, and after the recent sweeps by the *guardias* and the return of the herds south to the winter pastures order and tranquillity are restored around us: the provisions and firewood gathered throughout the summer and the supplies of meat smoked at the back of the cave (and in a few kitchens in Pontedo and La Llánava, which shall not be named), the sounds of the valley and the mountains, the monotonous rotation of sun and moon, the revolving shifts of *guardias* and our endlessly boring state of vigilance. Order and tranquillity are restored to everything except us. We are becoming more and more isolated and desperate, more and more fearful of the coming winter, which, as always, threatens to be long and ferocious and which will once again turn this damp hole into a squalid lair fit only for wild beasts.

Meanwhile, down below in the valley, the villagers have already started coppicing the poplars in order to ensure that there are tender leaves to feed the livestock when the forage from the orchards starts to grow thin. Down there, where the river has still not reached out to cover the riverbank with pools and marshes, a gentle sway of greenery in the distance betrays the swish of the pruning knife.

For several days this will be the only sound that reaches us from the valley, a faraway metallic swishing sound, which drifts over the tops of the poplar trees making them shiver with the cold and pain. A swishing sound that Ramiro and I have known since we were small boys when we joined our parents in the coppices, full of yellow leaves and stagnant water, to load the severed branches on to the cart.

That's why we're afraid of it, because we know it so well and we know that it is always accompanied by the first traces of snow. And because we also know that, for all that the villagers may fill their yards with firewood and leaves for the livestock, the winter's rage is implacable.

*

As evening falls Ramiro and I have finished greasing and loading the baits and traps; the wire snares for hares and the hard-steel trap with its sharp teeth – which Matalobos, the old wolf-trapper from Tejedo, gave us a couple of years ago – to catch any passing roe deer. The meat from a roe deer, cut into strips and smoked to preserve it, will help us fight off the last of the winter's hunger pangs.

They don't bring their sheep up from the villages any more by this time of the year. They keep them down in the stubble fields and the bogland lower down, rooting around in the alfalfa for the last autumn shoots, so there is no risk of the trap catching a stray sheep, revealing our whereabouts to the shepherds.

'The roe deer are still higher up, in the passes,' says Ramiro, with an air of satisfaction, as he checks the swish of the spring and the violent snap of the teeth crashing together. 'But you never know.'

The spring was stiff from the damp, almost seized up with rust. I had to scrape it painstakingly with my knife to remove the ruddy layer it had accumulated during its idleness and then grease it with hot tallow.

We scatter the snares across the hillside among the heather and thyme. We hide the deer trap in a swath of broom and cover it with dead leaves, so that we'll hear its violent, steely snap from the cave in the event that an unexpected visitor should become for ever imprisoned in its jaws.

*

'The wolf has come down as far as the Peña Negra already. It was howling all night.' Ramiro has brought out a bottle of brandy, and the two of us sit down at the entrance to the cave to watch as night falls once again. 'It won't be long before it snows.'

I take another slug from the bottle. The brandy has a violent, metallic taste. It's like the swishing sound of the trap or the wolves on the moonless horizon announcing the arrival of winter again.

Ramiro lights a cigarette and leans back against the cold face of the rock. 'Did you know, when I was young, before I went down the mine, I spent a couple of months with Ovidio, who lives up in the mountains, cutting wood in the Valdeón Valley, over there, by Riaño.' He points into the distance. 'They still hunt wolves over there like they did in the Stone Age, by corralling them. When they spot one they blow on a horn, and everyone comes out to join in the chase: men, women and children. I saw them do it once. No one is allowed to carry weapons, just sticks and tin cans. The strategy is to stalk the wolf and push him gradually towards a gully. At the end of the gully there's what they call the wolf-pit. It's a deep hole covered over with branches and leaves. When the wolf, finally, has gone into the gully, the men start to run behind it shouting and waving their sticks and the women and children jump out from behind the trees making a racket with their tin cans. The wolf gets scared and runs off straight ahead and falls into the trap. They catch him alive and for several days they parade him around the villages so that everyone can curse him and spit on him before he's killed.'

Ramiro is talking as though no one is listening to him. Ramiro is smoking and talking, but his gaze is lost in the mountains, fixed on the skyline where the sun is sinking down, corralled by the shadows into the bottomless pit of the freezing night.

*

In the morning a thin layer of frost is waiting for us on the hillside. A white layer that the feeble, bloodstained September sun, almost as cold as the frost itself, struggles to dissolve.

Now that the summer has gone, and with it our night-time excursions into the valley, Ramiro and I have sunk into an absolute tedium, permanently slumped on our bedding, with nothing to say to each other, nothing left to do except count down the hours by the distant whistle of the trains, or come to the mouth of the cave every now and then to watch the movements of the *guardias* through the binoculars, so it is always a special pleasure to go out as dawn breaks to check the snares and the deer trap.

You have to move carefully through the heather and thyme, looking for tracks in the frost and checking the small mounds of earth one by one. On any one of them you might find the grey bundle of a hare or the frightened stare of a badger still struggling to get free from its snare. But there's still nothing this morning. Only the silence, coiled like a blind animal in the undergrowth, and a cold wind gently blowing against our backs.

'It's a bad omen,' says Ramiro, disappointed, inspecting the last trap. It's what he always says on the first day, whatever we find. He looks around for non-existent tracks for a few moments, checks again that the snares are still working properly and heads back to the cave with a worried look on his face. 'It's going to be a harsh winter, Ángel.'

But tomorrow he'll be out again at dawn to check the traps, day after day, until finally, one morning, he'll come back and wake me up, his eyes shining in triumph and a bloodstained hare dangling from his fist.

12

I wake up, and I'm surprised by a strange glow in front of me. Ramiro's eyes are burning like coals in the darkness.

'What's wrong? Why are you looking at me like that?'

Now it's Ramiro who's surprised, as if my words had brought him around from a deep sleep. 'Nothing.'

But he's curled up very close to the fire, almost on top of it, and he's wrapped up in his cape and several blankets.

I sit up awkwardly on the bedding. 'Are you OK, Ramiro? You look as pale as a ghost.'

'I've got a fever,' he replies after a pause. 'That must be it.'

'Are you cold as well?'

'Yes.'

'Hang on,' I say, standing up. 'I'll put some more wood on the fire.'

'No, Ángel. Leave it,' he says. 'We'll have to put it out in a minute, it's daybreak already.'

As he's speaking the first threads of light from the new day shine in through the entrance to the cave, a new day that promises to be as cold and grey as the new month: November.

Ramiro gathers the blankets closer and leans his head against the wall, staring at the dying embers of the fire.

*

He's spent all day on his mattress, under his own blankets as well as mine, shivering.

Ramiro can't stop tossing and turning. He mutters a few stray words, incoherent, delirious. His face is gradually becoming deathly pale, making his feverish eyes stand out even more. I give him some fresh water and dampen down his forehead with a wet cloth, but it's no good. He's getting worse, and by midday his body is burning up with the fever.

Meanwhile, outside, a freezing-cold wind is ripping angrily through the broom and the heather, howling on the peaks of the mountain, forcing its way through the narrow entrance and right to the back of the cave and out again across the hillside, carrying off the frozen fire from Ramiro's eyes.

*

When night falls I stretch Gildo's cape over the mouth of the cave again and pile up dry branches in the pit we use for the fire. Soon a wave of heat spreads through the whole cave like a warm embracing hug.

We've been waiting for this moment since dawn.

'I'm going to make some coffee and put some brandy in it. It'll do you good.'

Ramiro doesn't even turn to look at me. 'Don't bother, Ángel,' he says.

'Why not?'

'It won't do any good.' He takes off his left boot and shows me a deep, inflamed wound running across the sole of his foot, tinged with purple, the flesh eaten away. 'It was a tin can,' he says. 'I was out walking barefoot yesterday, through the broom.'

'Why didn't you tell me earlier?'

'What for? What could you do?'

I find a saucepan and put water on to boil. I wash and clean the wound and bandage it up. But when I try to put his boot back on his foot is so swollen he can barely squeeze into it.

'You've got to see a doctor, Ramiro.'

He doesn't argue one way or another, he just looks at me in silence, from the depths of his feverish eyes. He can't see the wound and hasn't even tried to, lying there like a sack of potatoes on the mattress, but he must have guessed from my face that it's serious.

*

The Tojo Gorge, to the north of Vegavieja, is a deep valley, covered in gorse and ferns, where the River Negro begins. It's where the villagers have their winter shelters. They bring their cattle up here every winter to graze on the high pastures, so they can conserve the hay that they've stored up in their barns over the summer for later.

From high up on the mountain, in the night, the Tojo pastures look like stony stars in the inverted sky of the valley.

'There it is, down there.' Ramiro, wrapped in his cape and a blanket, points to the nearest winter shelter. 'There's a path that goes down by the river.'

'Sit down and rest a bit, Ramiro.'

But he refuses, testily. 'I'm not tired.'

And he starts walking again, leaning on my shoulder, hobbling.

*

A rich smell of dried, fermented grass permeates the stillness of the shelter. Alongside it the river rumbles in the night with an endless roar.

But the dog has already heard our footsteps and starts to bark from inside the shelter.

The barking gets louder when I knock on the side door, which is just next to the main door.

But it's the main door that opens a short while later. A woman's face, shocked and hostile, peers suspiciously through the crack. It's Tina, the woman who has taken Ramiro into her house and into her bed on so many nights.

'It's me, Tina. Don't be scared.'

She glances over to the nearby shelters, holding the dog between her legs and stroking it so that it won't bark, and closes the door again behind us.

The dog, a brindled mastiff, wearing a spiked collar around its neck to protect it from the wolves, growls softly as it watches us come in.

'What a shock you gave me,' says Tina, putting the bar back across the door.

Inside the shelter it's pitch black, and a warm smell of stables and straw gently hits the senses.

'Ramiro's ill,' I tell her.

'Ill? What's the matter, Ramiro?'

But he doesn't reply. Instead, we hear the rustling of straw.

Tina finds a paraffin lamp and lights it. The yellow glow lights up the outline of the cows as they lie at the end of the stable, and the dog's suspicious eyes from behind his mistress, and Ramiro's body slumped on the hay beside us.

'He's got a fever, a really bad fever, Tina. He cut his foot on a rusty tin.'

'Here,' she says. 'Help me put him on the bed.'

Between the two of us, we drag him over to the stuffed woollen mattress where she had been sleeping when we arrived. Ramiro is too weak to help, but Tina is very strong. She has the hard, chiselled strength of a single woman who has to live and work like a man.

'Wrap him up well. There're some more blankets over there.'

Tina wipes the sweat off his face with a rag. Ramiro is exhausted. We've been walking across the mountain for four hours without a break.

'Tina, I'm going down to the village, to find the doctor.'

'Don Félix?'

'Yes. Are you OK staying here with him on your own?'

Tina looks at Ramiro. His face is pale and contorted in the lamplight. The fever is eating him up. She wipes away the sweat again with the rag.

'Off you go. Don't worry. I'll look after him,' she says.

I wait for a little longer before leaving. I can't see any movement in the nearby pastures. The villagers and their animals must all be asleep, sharing the same space and warmth inside the shelters.

*

From a hiding place behind the oak trees lining the road I can see two bright lights leaving Vegavieja. It's the *guardias*. They go past, chatting, splashing in the puddles, setting off a host of dogs barking at them from the houses on the edge of the village.

I lie flat on the grass, holding my breath and with my submachine-gun at the ready.

'Shall we go up to Tejeda?'

'What, now?'

'It's only two o'clock.'

'No. Let's go down to Ferreras and kill some time at the mine. Who's going to be out and about on a night like this?'

'Just us!'

Their voices fade into the distance along the road, lost in the oak trees and the sound of splashing in puddles.

They don't realize that they nearly brushed the tip of my submachine-gun with their capes.

*

He's taken a long time to open the door. Too long for me to wait out in the open where I can be seen by any villager who can't get to sleep or caught in the sights of their shotgun.

The price on my head is now a hundred thousand pesetas, dead or alive.

When he finally appears, sleepy and half dressed, Don Félix peers out into the empty night with a look of surprise. From the top of the stairs, with his hand on the balustrade (one stone upon another) the elderly doctor looks fearfully into the shadows of the poplar trees and the tremor of the moon on the road.

He suddenly realizes that I am there.

*

'I asked you not to come back again.'

Don Félix has fetched his overcoat and comes out at the back of the house to meet me by the washbasin, in the empty stable covered in ivy where years ago he used to keep the horse on which he'd ride around the villages in the neighbourhood on his rounds. And where, one snowy night, by the light of a candle and helped by his wife, he extracted the bullet from my knee, which I got in the skirmish with the *guardias* the night we came down to La Llánava looking for Ramiro's brother.

But now Don Félix is retired, and he's getting on for seventy. All he asks is to be left in peace, to live out his final days tending the flowers in his greenhouse.

'I need your help, Don Félix. Otherwise I wouldn't have come.'

Don Félix stands there staring at me, his eyes hooded from fear and lack of sleep. Don Félix stands there staring at me as if he'd never seen me before in his life.

'Ramiro is sick,' I explain. 'He got a rusty tin stuck in his foot, and he's spent the whole day eaten up by fever. He's delirious. The wound looks really bad. It's black, like it's rotten. I'm scared he's got gangrene.'

But Don Félix's reply is curt and, perhaps, all the more so for being unexpected. 'I'm sorry, Ángel. I'm not a doctor any more.' He spoke without any expression, buried in his old overcoat, buried in the corner of his empty stable. 'I can't help you any more,' he says apologetically, and he looks away from me.

I search uselessly for the words that might persuade him. Then I suddenly understand that Don Félix had made up his mind years ago. He knows that the help he gave us in the past and the fact that he is old and weak will protect him from any reprisal by us. I also understand, although I'd prefer not to, that the year he spent in prison for helping me has filled his heart with fear.

Despite that, I still insist. 'Ramiro might die.'

But Don Félix doesn't even respond. He looks at me in silence with a blank expression. He watches me leave the stable without saying goodbye.

*

He catches me up on the road, still close to the village.

Don Félix is panting from the effort.

'Ángel.' I was just about to shoot at him but luckily I recognized him in time by his coat.

'Here, take this,' he says. 'Cut the wound open and wash it out with this.'

I take the bottle that Don Félix is holding out to me.

'What is it?'

'Alcohol,' he replies. 'There's nothing else you can do.' And then, already turning back towards home, he says, 'If you see the fever is getting worse and his foot is going black, hand him in as soon as you can. They'll have to amputate, and he won't be able to go on hiding.'

*

I am still close to the shelters, on the top of the hill that the path climbs before opening into the valley, when I hear the shots. First, a short, sharp burst. Then the violent racket of several guns firing at the same time, drowning everything else out.

Instinctively I hurl myself to the side of the road, landing in a puddle. I stay motionless for a few seconds, like a snake, with the submachine-gun at the ready and my face pressed down in the mud. I crawl into the undergrowth. I stop and listen again. I hear the shots clearly, close by, in the shelters.

The image of Ramiro burning up with fever sticks in my

memory, and I run uphill through wet gorse bushes that separate, silently, as I pass.

*

But I get there too late. It would have been too late anyway, however fast I ran. One man on his own with a submachine-gun and a couple of hand-grenades couldn't put up any real fight against all the *guardias* surrounding Tina's shelter. One man on his own with a submachine-gun and a couple of hand-grenades can't do anything except crouch among the gorse bushes and watch, as a dumb witness, the Dantean spectacle that is unfurling down there in the valley: the roof timbers, the door and gates, the hay in the barn, the whole shelter blazing in the night, transformed into a gigantic pyre. Red, violet and yellow flames bite with mercurial rage into the stone slabs and roof slates, spreading to nearby trees, leaping up through the roof and transforming the vault of the sky into an enormous melting pot. A dense column of black smoke fuses with the night, offering a barbarous, implacable god the brutalized baying of scorched cattle.

The *guardias* have stopped firing. Fanned out across the pastures, they must be waiting for Ramiro (and me as well, they probably think) to make a desperate break for it, but the seconds go by, slowly, and the painful silence from the shelter awakens a flicker of hope in my heart. Maybe Ramiro and Tina managed to get away in time and are now watching the fire and the cordon of *guardias* from the hillside, just as I am.

Suddenly, however, two gunshots ring out from the shelter. Crisp. Unmistakeable. Just a few seconds apart.

Almost immediately, the roof caves in, enveloped in flames.

Part Four
1946

13

I have been watching them all day. They came up at daybreak, along the road from Valgrande, and spread out across the top of the hillside rooting for fresh gorse and lavender shoots in the undergrowth, and now, herded together again, they are sleeping under the moon in the fresh pastures at Fuente Amarga.

I left the cave as the first shadows of the evening fell and began moving towards them. Slowly. Very slowly. Like a wolf trying to take a flock of sheep by surprise while they are innocently sleeping. But before I could get anywhere near them the horses sensed my presence and galloped away in a panic, leaving the herd of cows on its own and awakening deep inside me the terrible feeling that I've turned into a real predator. A predator that crawls under the weight of the night to steal a chicken from some sleepy yard or take a sheep that has become separated from its flock. A predator whose presence shocks both man and beast. A predator – or is there another word for it? – that only leaves its lair once the sunlight can no longer hurt its eyes, soaked in blood and solitude.

But today this predator has come down here in search of milk. Nothing else. Just a little bit of the milk that is swelling these cows' udders to bursting point and which the owners won't even notice when they get up to milk them tomorrow.

First I fill the clay jug that Gildo's wife left for me the other night by the cemetery wall at Candamo, full of olive oil. Then, exhausted after the tortuous climb down the Valgrande ravine through the heather, I lie down next to one of the cows on the warm straw to drink directly from its teats, slowly, like the snake that, one summer during my childhood, used to come into the stable behind our house at night and suckle the cows' milk. I still remember how terrified my sister and I were, hugging each other under the blankets, listening to the cows' distraught lowing as they called out to the snake the night my father discovered its nest in the hayloft and beat it to death with a hoe.

But I know that when they kill me not even the cows will mourn for me.

*

All through the night I watch the ancient dance of steel and grass, the green and black zigzag of death at my feet and the lonely glow of moonlight over Illarga. All through the night I have been bent double in the field with the scythe in my hands and the submachine-gun strapped across my back, so that at daybreak my family will find a freshly cut field.

It's my humble way of giving them back, anonymously, one of the many nights I've robbed from them over the years.

*

When I get back to the cave, as dawn is almost breaking, the silence comes out to greet me at the entrance. It has completely filled the passageway and is starting to invade the cracks in the rock and the deepest reaches of the broom like a dirty fog.

When Ramiro was still alive it was easy to escape from the

silence with an exchange of looks or words, but in this damp hole, where only silence has reigned since the beginning of time, not even the sound of a voice can now break its grip, the deep bellowing nestled in the depths of the mountain and in my heart.

It took me a long time to get used to it. At first I would toss and turn under the blankets, finding it impossible to bear the whole weight of solitude all by myself. I would wake up with a start in the middle of the night like a hunted animal, startled by its breath. Many a time I left the cave and wandered across the hillside for hours on end, aimlessly, senselessly, trying to erase how irrationally perfect it was until, gradually, I had to admit that I couldn't do anything to escape its presence and its company. Until, gradually, I had to admit that the silence was the only friend I had left.

Now the silence is my strongest ally in this long struggle against death, and it comes out to greet me at the entrance of the cave, like a dog, when I return.

*

I leave the jug of milk hidden in the broom, covered with a blanket to protect it from the light. I eat a bit of bread and dried beef and stretch out on the mattress fully dressed, exhausted.

Outside, along the peaks of the Peña Malera, the sun is about to break through.

*

I wake up when everyone down in the valley is asleep. It's siesta time, and a violent red sun, the colour of dried blood, is hanging up there in the sky, draping golden pyramids across the wheatfields and keeping everyone penned inside their houses. Not one sign of life breaks the reign of the shadows and silence; not one dog in the street, not a sound, not even the slightest quiver of net curtains in the half-open windows, in rooms where men and women will now be sleeping, soaking the sheets with perspiration and sex.

Just me on the hillside, looking through my binoculars, watching over as the villagers sleep. Just me, looking through my binoculars, sentenced to stay on watch while everyone else is asleep.

*

When I get back from having a wash, I bring back the jug that I left in the broom last night. My sister did some baking the other week and left me a couple of loaves, like she always does, hidden in the corner of the orchard, so I crumble a bit of dry bread into some of the milk and drink it. I pour the rest into empty tins so that it will curdle and ferment. It will not take long before it starts dripping, mysteriously, as it turns into cheese.

Afterwards, with no tobacco, like so many other times, I roll a cigarette with potato leaves, which I have dried out by the fire and I sit at the entrance to the cave to clean the weapons as I keep watch.

The valley has started to awaken, and an interminable succession of lowing and half-open doors spreads a deep beating pulse back across the villages, which had been briefly interrupted by the siesta. Teams of oxen, people and carts come and go along the roads, loading up cereals and slaving away in the fields. They all seem to be blinded by the sun and the incandescent glow of the rye. They all seem to be half asleep from the recent memory of the siesta and the dry rasping murmur of the threshing boards.

But, from time to time, they take a break to wipe away the

sweat and the straw dust and, almost without thinking, as if they'd been carefully trained, they look up at the hillside, scanning the heather and the oak trees for my distant, vigilant, silent presence.

*

They never stop thinking about me, not for a single moment. They've been after me now for nine years, and they're still searching for me. They don't even stop to blink. They won't stop until they see me, slumped on the roadside, with nettles growing out of my mouth and eyes.

This morning, when I went back to the cave, they were patrolling the road and the streets of La Llánava. Now they're searching along the railway line to Ferreras.

Evening falls, and another day melts away, like the frost on the peaks of the Peña Negra, but the *guardias* never stop thinking about me, not for one single moment.

14

The moon has become tangled in the branches of the poplar trees, and its faraway glow barely manages to light up the slow spiralling of the dancers or the couples stealing away in search of somewhere more private.

Close by to me, at the side of the road, a swarm of boisterous children mill around the large leather trunk that Braulio, the hawker from Tejeda, uses to display his magic world of sweets and sherbet. Further on, small groups of older men and women, dressed up in their Sunday best, watch the younger ones dance with an undefined mixture of nostalgia and envy.

It's been so long since I've been able to do this, just mingle with other people like an ordinary man, with nothing to mark me out as a creature apart. Here, in the shadows of the poplar trees, there's nothing to give away my true identity, and a sweet sensation gradually intoxicates my senses until I can even forget for a moment the silence of the cave and the deep despair of all the nights I have wandered aimlessly across the hillside. As if it wasn't me who'd come down to the fiesta at La Llera, attracted like a small child by the sound of the accordion biting the wind. As if it wasn't me who'd come here, driven by memories and loneliness.

It's a sweet sensation, which envelops me like a fog and which also blurs and dissipates at the point of contact between my hand and the gun. The feel of that cold grey metal in my pocket, which serves to remind me again of what I really am, here and now: a wolf among sheep, a strange and unfamiliar presence.

*

Those are not her eyes looking at me, they are two black embers.

The moon is high in the sky, and weariness is setting in as people start dispersing, heading back home, and Martina's eyes have reached through the shadows of the night in order to find their way eventually to mine.

I'd already spotted her some time ago, swirling in a cloud of blurred faces, indistinct faces twisted by the artificial light, in which it was still not difficult for me to discover some distinct memory of former pupils and neighbours. All of them now marked by the passage of years and oblivion. All inaccessible to me on the other side of destiny. All completely alien to my presence among them, incapable of even imagining (like the *guardias* standing next to the musicians, watching the dance with boredom written across on their faces) that I could dare to come here today.

Only Martina has recognized me. Only she has been able to discover, in among the shadows of the poplar trees, the man who danced with her, ten years ago now, in this very field with his arm tightly around her waist. The man who had arrived in the village as a schoolmaster, who spoke to her of love and raising a family. The man whom the dark whirlwind of war took away from her life for ever.

She stops for a moment, watching me, motionless, her eyes burning into mine.

Then (nobody has noticed) she carries on dancing, clinging tightly to her husband.

*

The accordion's music has pursued me even as far as the springs of the Peña Negra.

Even as far as the springs of the Peña Negra, Martina's eyes have carried on burning into mine.

*

They hid the truth from me until the last moment. They silenced their own grief in order to keep mine hidden until there was no longer any hope. Then my sister hung her yellow scarf in the window, and Pedro, her husband, came up the mountain to meet with me in the sheepfold on the pass.

Even they don't know exactly where the cave is.

I wait for him for almost an hour, here between the walls of the sheepfold, which the summer and the sheep abandoned only a week ago. I wait in the shadows, in the corner, nervously listening to the sounds of the mountain as I try to guess the reason for this sudden signal. Then, finally, the door opens with an ancient creak, and Pedro seeks me out in the darkness and tells me point blank. Exhausted, crushed by his years and tired of suffering, my father is dying, down there in the valley.

'Tonight, tomorrow, I don't know, Ángel. He's unconscious, breathing his last. The doctor says it's just a matter of hours now.'

Pedro looks nervously at the shadows around us in the sheepfold, short of breath, his voice clipped after the climb up the mountain. He leans back against the wall, trying to avoid my sudden icy stare. As if what is happening were all his fault. As if he were responsible for the news that has just lodged in my heart like a bullet.

Whereas all he has actually done is put his life in danger for me, once again.

'Juana wanted to tell you before, on Friday, when he first got bad,' he tells me after a pause. 'But what was the point? You've got enough to cope with.'

Through the broken roof, which is falling apart, eaten away by the snow, a shaft of damp light from distant stars creeps through at an angle, lighting up the eyes of this man whose desire to marry my sister could not be put off by risk or fear or the pressure and threats of the *guardias*. This man who has already begun to suffer the consequences of becoming part of my life.

'What do you think you'll do, Ángel?' Pedro is still leaning back against the wall, motionless in front of me, now looking at me again.

But I don't know how to reply. It's as if the silence, this hard transparent silence that always, inevitably takes hold of me at moments like this, has transformed my face into a cold, expressionless grimace and paralysed my tongue.

All I can do is shake my head when he asks me if I need anything.

He waits in vain for a response. I can't utter a word, not one word. A frozen heart is a landscape with no wind and no feeling.

Pedro stands up. He's getting more and more nervous, impatient to start off back home. 'I've got to go, Ángel. Juana's there on her own with him. She'll be worrying until I get back. Keep an eye on the window. We'll keep you posted.' Then, as he reaches the doorway, he says, 'I'm really sorry, Ángel. Especially for you.'

'Me?' My voice sounds like someone else's. My words sound as if I hadn't spoken them. As if they came from some faraway place to which I had never been.

'Juana's got me,' says Pedro, 'but now you've got nobody.'

*

On my way back to the cave in the middle of the night, tripping over the heather like a sleepwalker, the memory of my father explodes in my brain, shattering into a thousand pieces, into a painful avalanche of shrapnel or shards of broken glass, which can only just reach into my hidden pain before continuing into the bottomless mire of oblivion.

On my way back to the cave, the memory of my father becomes a shadow of the moon and heather and blood.

*

I can't stand it any more. I can't stand the anxiety of waiting and the echoing howl that whistles through the walls of my heart like the *cierzo* wind.

All day long I've watched the house, staring at the window, waiting for the long-distance signal that would tell me how my father was doing. All day long, crouched like a mole at the entrance to the cave, not eating or sleeping, without even bothering to keep an obligatory eye on the *guardias*, I've watched the regular comings and goings of neighbours to and from my house, trying to make out the expressions on their faces through the binoculars.

All day long I've watched in vain. No signal, no expression, nothing has broken the cordon of silence surrounding the walls of my house.

That's why, as soon as night falls, I pick up my submachine-gun, and, without a second thought, I head down the mountain.

*

There they are, as I feared, posted in the back alley, watching the house and waiting for me. Waiting for me to make the mistake of coming down to say goodbye to my father.

There are three of them, and they won't leave their posts until the dawn arrives with its cold light to relieve them.

But I haven't come this far to be barred from entering my own house. I haven't risked my life tonight in order to go back to the cave with my hands empty and this icy howl gnawing at my entrails.

I know that I've still got one option, only one option, which is so weak and risky that on another occasion I would have rejected it out of hand. But today, on the brink of madness, with my instincts and reason crumbling in the mists of despair, I'm ready to take my chances, come what may.

*

For a long while I crouch behind the trees, confirming what I'd suspected. As usual, the *guardias* are focused on the back entrance to the house. One on each corner and another one behind a wall, blocking off my path to the hayloft and the small window in the stable.

So I crawl slowly through the orchards towards the front of the house, cross the stream through the reed beds and then, like any other neighbour who's finished his supper and fed the cattle, I go and visit my father on his deathbed, walking confidently along the road and up to the front door. The *guardias* would never suspect, and certainly not on this night, that I'd enter my house through the front door.

That heavy old walnut door that I've not pushed open these last ten years.

*

Everyone has turned towards me, startled.

The murmured conversations and hushed prayers have stopped short and, like a sudden burst of snow, fear and silence have struck the walls of this room already touched by the sound of death.

Everyone has turned towards me as if death itself had just appeared behind me.

Standing by the door, with my submachine-gun lowered, I scan the room and see the silent, shocked faces of the women who are gathered in black around the bed like some religious painting, the bitter green glow of the oil-lamps, the distant looks of the men standing next to the window, the scent of lavender, my sister's eyes on the other side of the room next to the headboard where a cold flame bleeds on to the maroon blankets, lighting up my father's deep, staccato breathing. He's now completely cut off from everyone around him. He's now definitively sunk into that subterranean river that is flowing around his mouth and arms.

I don't even recognize the people who stand aside in silence to let me through. Their faces are blurred by a mist, while at the end of the room my father's face becomes clearer and larger, white with death on the white surface of the pillow.

'Father.' I take his hand in mine. It feels like a shard of ice. 'It's me, Ángel. I've come down to see you.'

'He can't hear you, Ángel.' It's my sister's voice. She is standing next to me, already dressed in black, her eyes brimming with tears.

But it's me who can't hear. It's me who can't understand the finality of her words and it's me who insists, squeezing my father's hand again and again, until it hurts.

'Father, it's me. I've come to see you. Can't you hear me? It's Ángel.'

'Go away, Ángel. For the love of God, get out of here. Leave him in peace!' Suddenly, Juana's voice has broken into an irrepressible howl, a scream that shakes the walls and the terrified faces of everyone in the room but which can't awaken my father, his eyes gripped by a deep white sleep. 'What exactly do you want? Are you trying to finish him off?'

*

There was a cloudburst around midnight. There was a cloudburst like it would never be daytime again.

But the new day broke with a cold, milky light, with a light steeped in ozone and muddy grey slime that lit up my house and, in the window, the denial of the wind that can never leave me again.

*

At midday, now the rain has eased off and the mud has taken over the river and the paths, the sound of the dogs barking and the church bells in La Llánava reach out to me at the back of cave, in the freezing-cold corner where I have spent hours trying uselessly to forget the barking of this dog that is feeding on my blood, inside my heart.

In front of my house people wait under their umbrellas for

my father to make his final exit. They are like black shadows, blurred in my binoculars by the rain and the distance. Faraway shadows who will surely be commenting on what the whole village knows by now, that I was there last night, that while they were sleeping, while the wind was beating against their windows and the dogs were howling in the stables sensing the arrival of death, I left my hiding place in the depths of the woods, crossed the concentric circles of the night and oblivion and turned up unexpectedly at my father's house to say my last goodbyes to that man who is now being carried out on the shoulders of his neighbours, never to return.

The bells have begun to toll with an even heavier sadness. Their damp peals tremble over the rooftops and the fields before dissipating with a metallic pain against the frozen mountains. The rain falls in a sudden burst of strength while the cart with the coffin starts to move off outside my house, dragging behind it a wake of umbrellas and the legend of that indomitable and invisible man who last night, once again, managed to make a mockery of the *guardias'* stake-out and who, no doubt, will be watching them from somewhere right now. That man they think about so many nights, in the heat of their stables and kitchens, as immortal as his shadow, as distant as the wind – brave, sharp, intelligent, invincible.

That man who, mirrored in the rain, on the mountainside, reflects the memory of what he has always been: a solitary, hunted man. A man hemmed in by fear and vengeance, hunger and the cold. A man who is even denied the right to bury the memory of his loved ones.

*

By the time I get to the road the rain has stopped. A distant grey moon gently lights up the outline of the mountains and the shivering trees. 'Look, Ángel, look at the moon. It's the sun of the dead.'

The river tears down the mountain, rough and furious. Its roar crashes against the trunks of the poplar trees and the black roofs sleeping in the distance, between the broken branches, their backs turned on the lonely orchard overgrown by nettles and silence since the beginning of time.

The gate is locked. An iron padlock hides beneath its rust the sleep of those who have already crossed the river of oblivion. But the wall is not very high. A crunch of brambles greets me on the other side and gently flattens me into the mud.

Here they are at last, grey and silent in front of my boots, the piles of mud where time ferments, where ancient passions and memories gently rot. Here they are, their graves like mountains of sadness beneath a distant, watery moon. My mother, buried next to the gates, the earth now hardened by the passing of the years. María, only there to give me her solitude and vengeance; Benito; Teresa, the little girl who drowned; Ramiro, in the outlaws' corner, now completely overgrown with nettles, after his charred body was paraded through the villages like a hunting trophy.

And there too, in front of my boots, still unnamed, still undated, the patch of earth where, since this afternoon, my father has been waiting for me.

'It's me. Ángel. I've come down to see you.'

15

'Take off those clothes. You're soaked through.'

Lina has turned the light out and locked the doors to the street.
Now she is poking around in the embers of the fire, and a glimmer
of red begins to glow at the back of the fireplace, lighting up her
hard, sleepy face. She'd already gone to bed.

'Where's the boy?'

'He's asleep. Keep your voice down.'

Lina puts my boots in the oven and spreads my clothes and
cape out to dry by the fire. Then she brings me a pair of trousers
and a shirt, which are much too big.

'They were Gildo's,' she says.

Gradually I start to warm up. Gradually, I start to rip from
my soul the imprint of the fog, which cuts through the November
night out there with its frozen knife.

Lina, her hair loose, wearing a white nightgown, sits down
next to me on the end of the bench. She's very pale, and she's
lost weight. Her face is a sea of endless wrinkles, etched deeper
by sleepiness, but perhaps that actually accentuates even more
the strange, tough beauty of this woman who is now approaching
the milestone of forty years of age completely on her own.

This woman who has never abandoned me, even in the most
difficult of times.

'How are you, Ángel?'

'I'm tired. More and more tired.'

'Winter's here already. It won't be long before it snows.'

The water drips from my clothes on to the fire surround, creating droplets of steam, white bubbles that vanish on the iron-work before they are even born. Like gaps in the fog. Like my voice in the grey silence of this kitchen.

'I'm not sure how much longer I can hold out.'

'Do you know what?'

'What?'

'Do you know what people are saying?' Lina shifts her position, shuffling uncomfortably on the bench. She avoids my eyes as she speaks. 'They're saying that the best thing you could do is swallow a bottle of brandy and put a bullet in your head.'

She's staring at me as if her heart has stopped beating, as if shocked at what she has just said to me. As if she's shocked at herself. She's staring at me as if this is the first time she has ever set eyes on me. Before leaving the room she puts a blanket over me and pokes the dying embers one last time. I had fallen asleep.

'I'll call you at five. Sleep well.'

'Lina.'

'What?'

'Tell them that I'm not a dog. Tell them, Lina.'

Stretched out on the bench I can hear her footsteps going upstairs, the creaking of the floorboards above the kitchen, the sound of the bed as she climbs in. Stretched out on the bench I listen for a while to her deep, lonely breathing, and, I don't know why, I go to sleep with a brooding sense of betraying the memory of the man whose clothes I'm wearing.

*

Near the Fuente Amarga, by the isolated tile factory at Respino, the smell of burning stops me in my tracks. I stop walking and hold my breath. It's a smell of smoke in the distance, dissipated into the threads of fog.

From the vantage point of a rock and with my submachine-gun at the ready I sniff the solitude of the night like a wolf and listen intently to the sounds of the mountain around me. But the fog wipes everything out, blurring and jumbling up all the sounds and smells into one single fibre. It breaks down distances with a phantasmagorical roar.

It's impossible to know where the smell of burning is coming from, impossible to guess the direction of the smoke.

Some shepherd must have built a fire somewhere.

*

It was further up the hillside, beyond the fields of broom and the oak trees alongside the path, where a cloud of thicker smoke, blacker and more defined, made me drop down into the heather, flattening myself against the ground on to the frozen-solid couch grass. There isn't any campfire burning, faraway and isolated, beneath the fog. There aren't any shepherds or muleteers keeping themselves warm on the hillside. The fire is right here in front of me. The fire is right here in the ravine, and the smoke is pouring out of the hidden mouth of the cave.

All of a sudden my submachine-gun has ceased to be a simple fountain of death, ready to kill. All of a sudden my submachine-gun has become a metallic flash of lightning racing towards the oak trees, fleeing from the exposed position on the hillside. It spreads a trail of leaves under the red frost. Between the clusters of broom it uncovers the compromised markers I set up yesterday when I left the cave. That branch I left over the path is no longer there. That line of leaves has been trampled over. That pile of soil that is no longer there must have been carried away on someone's boot…

The gunshot cuts through the threads of fog like a release of breath. It smashes into the mountain just in front of me, almost on top of me.

The gunshot cuts through the threads of fog and my heartstrings at the same time. But before I even realize it, even before the men who have been waiting for me have time to react, I am already rolling down the cliff face, dragging bits of scrub and loose rocks with me, bouncing down the slope like just another stone. Broken branches crash alongside me and push me onwards. The thistles and heather snatch at my clothes, trying to stop me. But there's no choice. The slope goes on and on. The slope never ends. The shots screech past me, searching out my shadow, and the shouts of the *guardias* tear at the fog around me. They are right here, their breath almost mingling with mine. They are right here. There's no choice.

My fall seems to go on for an eternity, never ending. Time has stopped indefinitely in my heart. There is only the black, frozen fog. Only the fog covering everything and, at last, a sharp, brutal thud under my feet. I run with all my strength. I run full of rage like a wounded dog, holding in the pain.

Down the mountainside, across the scrubland, breaking through the fog, I run with all my strength until I collapse from exhaustion at the bottom of the valley on the riverbank among the thick and freezing vegetation on which the first sprinkling of morning dew is glistening.

*

I can hear shouting, and I can just glimpse the shadows of birds. I can hear a gust of wind through the hazel trees and the fleeting sound of falling leaves.

I listen. I gently lift up my head, between the bulrushes and reeds. I look around. There is nothing, only silence, fog, strands of algae tangled together in the middle of the river and my own reflection in its depths.

Not a trace of the *guardias*. Not a shadow. Not a sound. Not even the muffled echo of a footstep or a voice.

But I can't move from here until nightfall.

*

The storm has lasted two days and two nights. Two days and two nights fleeing across the hills in the thick of the snow, always heading north. Towards the outer limits of the wind and solitude.

It started mid-afternoon, while I was still down by the river. A dry blast of wind blew away the last traces of fog through the hazel trees, and a deep roar came down from the mountains, dragging with it clumps of broom and broken branches. The strands of algae screamed furiously downriver, and a white sheet of steel and ice blocked out everything around me.

Across the four corners of the earth, in advance of the night and the winter, in advance of the stars and the dead and their prayers, it suddenly began to snow.

The storm has lasted two days and two nights. Two days and two nights fleeing across the hills, blinded by the wind, with no food or sleep, not knowing where to hide, where to go, motivated only by my own endless, inexhaustible desperation. This passion, which has dragged me far away from the smouldering remains of the cave. This passion, which has pushed me through the snow-storm and guided me in the darkness, avoiding the dangerous backlight on the hillsides and slopes, blending me into the snow under a white blanket that I stole from a yard in Vegavieja, walking backwards during the day to muddle my trail and confuse the *guardias* who, knowing that I've lost the shelter of my cave and thinking that I'm surrounded, will be watching all the villages and roads and scouring the mountains in a massive hunt which they hope, which they've been hoping for such a long time, will be the final one.

The storm has lasted two days and two nights. Now the third day is breaking. Maybe for me it will be my last day ever.

*

I wait for almost an hour without moving a muscle. The storm has been followed by a deep calm, and from a distance, under my white blanket, no one could make me out against the snow.

All around me an unreal and desolate landscape marks out the infinite reaches of silence. There's a metallic light that seems to come from nowhere, and up here, surrounded by the mountains, the horizon has disappeared, rubbed out again by the fog.

One movement by me, the slightest movement, would be enough to break this perfect balance.

But that is not what is keeping me here lying in the snow like a dead animal. It is not the blurred hallucination of the woods floating in the distance like phantasmagorical armies of ice that has kept me lying still, staring at the sky, for nearly an hour. It's exhaustion from walking for days non-stop and, more than anything, the final confirmation of a presentiment I had already felt in my dreams. My frozen beard and fingernails ripped by the cold, the transparent greyness that the dampness of the river and the snow have imbued into my breath and bones. The fear of discovering, as soon as I move, a numbness in a part of my body that the ice might have put to sleep for ever.

But I can't stay here indefinitely. I have to go on. I have to get up and start walking again in search of some place, an abandoned shelter, a cave or a farmhouse, where I can hide until my pursuers give up the hunt.

Gingerly, I reach under the blanket and cape to feel for any sensation in my hands, my legs and my feet. My clothes are frozen with a strange rigidity. My boots are now just two solid masses of damp and rigid leather. Slowly I rub my whole body with a dull indecision. My muscles contract without any strength or pain. But they are alive. All of them. They wake up gradually from a deep sleep, from a sleep so remote that it can't even reach my heart. I get to my knees like a beast that's fallen over, and I take another look at the shadows and outlines that delineate the silence. Nothing. Just me and the solitude. The solitude and the *cierzo* wind and the leafless lament of the snow, which I rub on my hands and face to get them to react.

I stand up with infinite sluggishness. My whole body groans like a cold, rusty machine. But I must go on. I must start walking again.

*

Towards midday I discover a shepherd's cabin at the foot of the mountain. The storm has destroyed the roof, and the fences around the corral are covered in snow. But, despite this and the fact that I've been walking since dawn without any sense of direction whatsoever, it's not hard to recognize the old shepherd's cabin at Láncara.

Slowly, sliding from tree trunk to tree trunk through the beech grove that leads down to the valley, I make my way towards the cabin. The snow around and about is hard and brilliant white, and there are no footprints. The *guardias* have not yet come to search here.

But my footprints are crisp and deep and could attract them at any moment.

*

Nightfall.

Another day fades away into the blue confines of the mountains like the *cierzo* wind.

Another day spent running away from myself with no rest and no hope.

*

I haven't even stopped to check all the places where the *guardias* are usually posted: the bridge over the river, the ford where the cows cross, the alleyway behind my house. All I can think of is getting there, escaping from the snow, collapsing anywhere like a sack of potatoes. For several days now the close proximity of death hasn't worried me in the slightest. For several days now I've even started to secretly yearn for it.

Broken, exhausted, barefoot, I walk through the deserted streets of La Llánava, carrying my boots in my hand to avoid the dogs' watchful insomnia and to muffle the sound of my footsteps. My feet are like two white bags, with no toenails, swollen up out of all proportion. My body can scarcely support the weight of my cape and blanket. Only anger keeps me on my feet, only anger and desperation, which give me enough bitter strength to drag myself inexorably towards my house. Towards that house where I don't know who will be waiting for me.

But there at last is the locked side gate leading to the hayloft, which on so many nights has guillotined the moon behind me. There at last is the cows' invisible breath, warm and heavy in its ancient depth, as comforting as a hug, both familiar and strange at the same time. It's a long while now since I've come to enjoy the company of my fellow man less than the company of animals. It's been a long time since I worked out exactly the place that they had reserved for me. But today, more than ever, after nine days of solitude and cold, solitude and hunger, I know how immensely human the simple warm darkness of a stable can feel.

I climb over the side gate with my last bit of strength. The straw groans softly. It's rotten and white. Like my feet. Like my soul.

Like the frozen night, which the side gate has rubbed out behind me for ever.

16

I open my eyes, and I can't see anything. Or, rather, the darkness is even thicker and blacker than the actual darkness of sleep.

I move my arms and legs and feel a weight bearing down on them closely. As if I had died and the invisible dimensions of my body were framed by an earthy coffin.

But it's not true. I know it's not true. I know that this illusory feeling is just the last gasp of sleep. Despite the darkness, despite the close and suffocating pressure of the earth, I know that I am still alive, completely alive, at least as alive as when I was still wandering through the snow like the wind. Although for the past month I've not been able to see any light or hear the winter's blue language. Although for the past month, stretched out like a mole in this underground tomb that Pedro and I dug out in the pen where we keep the goats, between the stables and the bakery, I have been much closer to the world of the dead.

I've been woken up by the sound of the door opening and a scuffle of hooves on top of the wooden board covering me. I listen out. Footsteps and a low voice cutting a path between the goats and the silence. I hold my breath, completely still. I've no idea what the time is. I don't even know if it's day or night outside. I don't know how long I could have been asleep.

But there's nothing to worry about. At last I hear the agreed signal: three sharp knocks on the board.

When I get out of the hole my sister or brother-in-law have already gone. They've left me some food in a saucepan, hidden in the dry leaves, and they've gone, locking the door from the outside.

They do the same thing every night when everyone in the village has gone to sleep.

The goats' eyes are full of surprise, like black streaks of lightning, as they watch me leave the hole. They still haven't got used to my presence. They mill around uncomfortably, seeking out the protection of the walls. They jump out of my way as if I were an apparition.

I sit in a corner on a bale of hay, eating my supper. In front of me a gentle light shines obliquely over the pen through the courtyard window. Gradually my eyes get accustomed to it. Gradually my whole body starts to loosen up after my enforced immobilization.

*

Even I could not have imagined what a man who is alone, completely alone, sitting in a corner or walking around among the goats, is capable of thinking about over the course of a night.

Not even God himself could ever know what a man who is alone, completely alone, bitterly alone, is capable of wishing and begging for over the course of a night.

A soul alone, in the middle of the night, is always in torment.

*

It's daybreak. The bells ring out, calling in the flock, and a train passes by in the distance, the sound melding with the *cierzo*. The light becomes whiter and steadier through the window overlooking the yard.

The time has arrived. The time has arrived to go back into that airless hole and stretch out like a mole under my wooden board. The time has arrived to come face to face again with the stinking breath of the magma and the rotten lichens that impregnate the entrails of the earth and the hearts of those who encroach upon their territory.

It's daybreak. In a few minutes my sister or my brother-in-law will come in search of the goats and will spread the manure over the wooden cover. Then I will become a dead man again.

*

At first it was a confused sound, far off in the courtyard, coming from the direction of the hayloft and the stable. Then there was a menacing silence, charged with tension. Finally, after interminable minutes of nervously waiting, the sound of the door bursting open and, right above me, the trample of voices and boots and scrabbling goats.

If immobility and silence have always been permanent and compulsory for me inside the tomb, now, in contrast, suddenly, they've become an integral part of my own identity. If anxiety has always accompanied me and followed me wherever I go like a dog, now, in contrast, suddenly it has become the only thing that drives me on. The sound of the *guardias'* boots comes and goes above the board, as they kick the goats out of the way. They shout and use their weapons to threaten my sister and brother-in-law, who they've probably forced to go out in front of them into the courtyard like they always do, just in case I'm hidden there and open fire out of the darkness. Even though I can't see them, I can follow their movements with absolute precision from their words and shouting. They rummage through the stacked-up bales of hay, pull aside piles of firewood and sacks of provisions, poking in every corner. Finally, they bang the floor and walls with their rifle butts, searching for the hidden recess that the board, once again, is hiding from them just centimetres above me.

They've searched the whole house a thousand times, every last corner – the stables and hayloft, the goat pen, the bakery, the kitchen, the bedrooms, the attic – a thousand times without ever finding the slightest trace of me.

A door slams violently. The voices go off towards the back of the courtyard. The goats settle down and silence descends on me again. Once again. For how long? How long will I have to carry on living like this?

*

Half an hour later, barely half an hour, the door to the pen opens again. Gently. It opens gently this time and, unlike the other times, I hear three sharp knocks above me.

Juana helps me lift the board from the outside. Her eyes are blazing and her shaven head is the first thing my eyes focus on.

'What happened? What did they do to you, Juana?'

Juana doesn't reply. She leaves the board to one side and takes a few steps back, in between the goats, into the darkness.

'They beat you, didn't they?'

She shakes her head absurdly. The bruises and the marks of blows on her face speak out unequivocally on her behalf.

The goats, as always, back away from me in shock. Far from getting used to me, every day that goes by they recoil even more from my company and, recently, they no longer even dare come up to the edge of the board. My scent of damp earth frightens them. My deathly pallor fills them with suspicion and terror.

'What about Pedro?'

'They've taken him away.' Juana is sunk into the darkness. She looks at me, motionless and far away among the goats, as if she is frightened of me, too. 'Are you hungry?'

'No.'

'I couldn't cook you anything,' she says. 'The *guardias* arrived suddenly in the afternoon.'

'Don't worry, Juana. I'm not hungry.'

While I've been down there below it's started to snow again. The courtyard is completely covered, and a frozen glow coming through the window hurts my eyes. The year is drawing to a close and does so, as always, with a rare savagery. I don't know which is worse: to be buried down here, suffocating under the board and the constant searches by the *guardias*, or coping with the fury of another winter on the mountain.

'Ángel.' Juana's voice is broken and trembling, split by the strain and pressure of living at breaking point. Right from the start, since she came into the pen and sought me out under the board, before the *guardias* could even have left La Llánava, I knew that something awful had happened or that she had something awful to tell me, something that I could never imagine as I wait with my back to her looking through the window at the solitude of the courtyard.

'You've got to leave here, Ángel.'

For a few seconds I didn't even understand what my sister had said. For a few seconds I wasn't even aware that I had heard her words. They stayed there floating in the air, suspended behind me, until the silence, powerful once more, flooded the pen like vomit and made them disintegrate.

'You've got to leave here.'

Slowly I turn around to seek out my sister's outline. Slowly my eyes penetrate the darkness again. 'Where can I go, Juana? Where?'

We are standing face to face, separated by the hole in the ground and the warm darkness of the pen. Juana is motionless and remote, like just another shadow among the shadows of the goats. I am pale as death in her eyes in the thin grey light from the window.

We are standing face to face, remote, not looking at each other, not speaking to each other, as if we were no longer brother and sister.

Until Juana, suddenly broken, suddenly drowning in rage and tears runs out of the pen, runs away from me and from her own words into the lonely snow-filled courtyard.

*

I found out the next day that Pedro came back home at dawn. The *guardias* had taken him up to the Candamo Mountains and put him through a mock execution.

I found out the next day that Pedro soaked it all up like he always does without breathing a word.

*

Juana is right. Juana and everyone else who, so many times over all these years, has told me again and again, 'You have to leave here, Ángel. This land is unforgiving. This land is cursed for you.'

I have to leave here, yes. But where do I go? And, above all, how?'

If I knew the answers I would have escaped a long time ago

without anyone having to tell me. Without having to hear that maybe the best thing for me would be to swallow a bottle of brandy and put a bullet in my head. Without having to hear my sister tell me something that (and I know this is true as well) hurt her more than it hurt me. This sentence has lasted too many years. Too many years of arrests and searches, beatings and insults, isolated in fear from our own neighbours. Oh yes. Too many years suffering for this man, this lost cause who is desperately gripping on to life and who, in his desperation, is dragging his loved ones down with him.

Juana is right. I can't stay here for ever, laid out on my back like a corpse with no light and no hope, staring into the void with an empty heart. I have to get away, break this vicious circle that each day pushes me a little bit closer to suicide. I have to escape from this cursed land and put kilometres of silence and oblivion between me and the memory of me, between me and this tomb where the heat and desperation fuse together into one putrefied substance that is starting to spread through my body. Like that man from Nogales who, when the war was over, while Ramiro, Gildo and I were wandering across the mountains, hid himself under a feeding trough in his stable and didn't come out again for six years, by which time he was blind and sick and wasted away, so his wife had to bury him again in the night, furtively, in a corner of the garden.

Juana is right. Juana and everyone else who, so many times over all these years, has told me again and again there is no hope or forgiveness for me here.

All that is left for me here is a slow death, buried alive.

The light hurts my eyes after all this time. This sad, icy sunlight burns with the brightness of snow. After so many days without being able to feel the light on my skin, just like feeling nostalgia or the rain. The light hurts and stains my senses, which have been darkened by the night, rubbed out by the wind, drowned in my sister's eyes when she closed the door behind me, almost certainly never to see me again.

Gradually the light has sketched the outline of the old railway station at Ferreras against the moribund darkness of the night. The snow-covered roof, the lonely platform, the tracks eaten away by rust and ice. Gradually the light has diluted the cloud of steamy breath emerging from my mouth in short bursts. I have walked for four hours across the mountain to get here. Four hours in the middle of the night, completely alone, completely in the dark, without the strength even to look over my shoulder or to wish for daybreak to come. As if time had stopped for ever within the four walls of my house. As if the desperation and fear that flooded my memory in that tomb day and night had dissolved like dust upon contact with the wind.

But now day is breaking in the old railway station at Ferreras. Day is now breaking, and this light that hurts my eyes and blinds me is also waking up my hearing: the crunch of my boots in the snow, the invisible dogs freezing outside, the howl of the breeze along the empty platform. And that faraway metallic sound that slowly starts to approach. Slowly.

*

The handful of travellers looked at me sleepily rather than showing any surprise. Maybe they were puzzled by my deathly pallor from the days I spent underground and the obvious age of these boots and this overcoat which once belonged to my father and which are now travelling with me on this long journey into oblivion or death. Maybe they were puzzled by my nervous silence. But they barely glanced at me, distant and without surprise, and then carried on dozing in their seats.

I look for my own seat by the window, near the door. I leave my suitcase on the floor between my legs and, once I'm sitting down with my cap pulled down over my eyes, I mentally check my luggage, which I cannot declare: the money sewn into my overcoat lining, the false documentation, the handgun, which is trembling like ice between my fingers in my pocket, and the crumpled map, hidden in my boots, which is all I have to guide me across the border through the hills and the night. The bell has rung on the platform. Cold. Dissipated by the wind. And the train has started moving off very slowly. Gradually, through the frozen, misted-up window, I watch the old station building and the deserted platform disappear. Gradually, through the frozen, misted-up window, I watch through the trees as the snow-capped mountains of Illarga fade into the distance. The mountains where nine years of my life and the unforgettable memory of my dead friends will remain for ever. I look around me. Everyone is asleep. I curl up under the heavy raincoat. I lean my head against the back of the seat. All I can hear now is the cold black rumbling of the train that is pulling me away. All I can see now is snow.

AFTERWORD:
MY CHILDHOOD HERO
HAS DIED

On 6 April 2004 Casimiro Fernández Arias died in exile in France. He was the last survivor of the resistance fighters from the central mountain region of León after the Civil War. He had never returned to live in Spain.

Together with his brothers and his comrades he was the inspiration for my novel *Wolf Moon*. Casimiro was born at the start of the twentieth century in La Mata de la Bérbula, a village near Valdepiélago, in the Curueño Valley, León. Although he came from a very humble farming background, he chose to become a miner like his two brothers and was working in the Matarrosa del Sil mines in El Bierzo when the Civil War broke out on 18 July 1936.

He was twenty-four years old at the time and had already joined the anarchist union CNT (the Confederación Nacional del Trabajo, or the National Confederation of Labour). He enlisted with the Republican army and fought in their ranks first in León, in the Cármenes sector, and later in Asturias, where he was caught out by the collapse of the northern front in the autumn of 1937.

Taking refuge in the mountains along with many others, Casimiro ended up leading a group of fugitives who survived for nine years trapped in the Curueño and Torío Mountains. The group included his two brothers, Andrés (who would soon be murdered) and Amable, as well as two of his cousins from his home village, Gonzalo and Laurentino, and a shifting number of other resistance fighters from both Asturias and León. Everyone who knew him spoke of his bravery and calm manner. His group was known collectively as 'the Arias', after the surname shared by the three brothers, and in the summer evenings of my childhood – which I spent, like them, in La Mata de la Bérbula, in my grandparents' house – I was told hundreds of stories about them, mythologized by the popular imagination, which I eventually gathered up into my first novel, *Wolf Moon*.

While I was working on the novel in the early 1980s Casimiro came back to La Mata one summer. He hadn't been back for forty years, not since he had managed to escape to France together with the surviving members of his group. He returned once more, as far as I recall, when the novel had been published and had even been turned into a film. I remember because I watched the film with him and Calixto, another member of the Leonese Maquis who had returned from exile by then, together with Julio Sánchez Valdés, the film's director. It was a video copy, and we watched it in a café in Cistierna. Although he was only in Spain for a short while I made good use of the time to record several hours of interviews with him and to join him as he returned to the places in which he had gone through so much. I can recall several anecdotes from those days, but I shall recount only one. It took place in Correcillas, a small village in the parish of Torío, lost up in the mountains, where

Casimiro and his comrades had had one of their safest hideouts and where so many of the stories about them – which I had been told when I was gathering information about the resistance fighters – were based. We arrived there at noon one midsummer's day. At the entrance to the village there were several women washing clothes by the river. Casimiro stopped and stared at them.

The women greeted us with a 'Good morning', but Casimiro did not reply. He simply looked around. (What could be going through his head, I wondered, coming back here to this village where he had lived through so much more than half a century ago?) The women looked at us with a mixture of surprise and suspicion. They seemed to be asking, just by looking at us, who on earth were these two strangers coming to our village in the middle of nowhere and standing there staring in silence.

'I'm a traveller,' replied Casimiro after one of them, the eldest, finally asked.

'And where are you from?' was her next question.

'I don't have a homeland,' said Casimiro, smiling, as the women looked astonished and increasingly intrigued.

The situation was becoming a bit awkward, with Casimiro standing there looking at the women without saying a word (and I, naturally, did the same) when suddenly he asked, 'Is so-and-so still alive?' (I say so-and-so because I've forgotten the name of the villager after whom he was asking, but it turned out to be the father of the woman he'd been speaking to.) It was as if he had given a password. The woman dropped what she was doing, dried her hands on her apron and rushed over in tears to hug Casimiro, to the astonishment of the other women, who didn't have a clue what was going on. What was going on was very simple. Only someone from the past, from the deepest reaches of history, could have asked after a villager who had died forty years ago. And that someone could only have been Casimiro, the man her father had helped on numerous occasions and for whom she herself had knitted so many socks when she was a teenager and the post-war years filled the villages with hunger and fear, as I had been told more than once as I went around the villages in the region, dredging for stories about the resistance fighters.

That day Casimiro and I ended up half drunk. The whole village wanted to welcome us with open arms and buy us a drink, apart from one man who ran away to hide as he had done in the past when the resistance fighters arrived in Correcillas. 'Tell him I won't hurt him now. I don't carry a gun any more,' said Casimiro with a smile when he found out. We received the same welcome many more times as we went around the villages where Casimiro and his comrades (all of them dead by then apart from his brother Amable, who would die a short time later in France) had been the protagonists in so many stories and had suffered so many ordeals.

That was the last time I saw him. We exchanged a couple of letters and spoke on the phone on a few occasions, but I never saw him again. Two years ago, when I was on a visit to Toulouse, I went to see him in Crançac, the town in Aveyron where he lived with his wife, who was also the daughter of Spanish exiles. Much to my disappointment he had gone to visit his daughter in northern France, and I could only speak to him on the telephone. And now that it's too late I regret not keeping in touch with him more than I did, not talking more to that man who ended up without a homeland at such a young age, who unwittingly played the leading role in the stories of my childhood dreams and who, in the fullness of time, would inspire the novel in which I tried to recount those stories.

Julio Llamazares
2004

THE STORY OF PETER OWEN PUBLISHERS

Peter Owen founded his eponymous publishing house in 1951. From the beginning he championed major but little-known international authors including Hermann Hesse, Shusaku Endo, Anaïs Nin and Tarjei Vesaas, often publishing them in English for the first time. Hesse's Siddhartha *was one of the first novels he published, buying the rights for £25. The company helped to build the British writer Anna Kavan, as well as Margaret Crosland, who published 25 books with the firm – translating 18 titles from the French, including works by Jean Cocteau and the Marquis de Sade, as well as writing seven books of her own. Peter Owen also published Salvador Dalí's only novel. The list eventually included ten Nobel Prize-winning authors, earning Owen an OBE for services to literature.*

Born in Nuremberg in 1927, Owen moved with his British-born mother to London soon after Hitler came to power; his German-Jewish father joined them a year later. His first job was as an office boy at The Bodley Head, and, after a brief stint in the RAF, he used an armed-forces paper quota and capital of around £800 to set up his own publishing company, aged 24. Several years later, an aspiring novelist named Muriel Spark came to work for him as editor.

Peter Owen was one of a kind; a maverick, a pioneer. Throughout his seven decades in publishing he was known as much for his flamboyant shirts and snakeskin ties as for his dogged persistence and dedication to high-quality literature in translation. Independent to the end, Owen ran his publishing house until he died in 2016, aged 89. His memoir, Not a Nice Jewish Boy, *appeared shortly after his death. Pushkin Press acquired the company in 2022.*

AVAILABLE AND COMING SOON FROM PUSHKIN PRESS CLASSICS

The Pushkin Press Classics list brings you timeless storytelling by icons of literature. These titles represent the best of fiction and non-fiction, hand-picked from around the globe – from Russia to Japan, France to the Americas – boasting fresh selections, new translations and stylishly designed covers. Featuring some of the most widely acclaimed authors from across the ages, as well as compelling contemporary writers, these are the world's best stories – to be read and read again.

MURDER IN THE AGE OF ENLIGHTENMENT
RYŪNOSUKE AKUTAGAWA

THE BEAUTIES
ANTON CHEKHOV

LAND OF SMOKE
SARA GALLARDO

THE SPECTRE OF ALEXANDER WOLF
GAITO GAZDANOV

CLOUDS OVER PARIS
FELIX HARTLAUB

THE UNHAPPINESS OF BEING A SINGLE MAN
FRANZ KAFKA

THE BOOK OF PARADISE
ITZIK MANGER

THE ALLURE OF CHANEL
PAUL MORAND

SWANN IN LOVE
MARCEL PROUST

THE EVENINGS
GERARD REVE